THE
MERMAID
MURDER

A BROWN AND DE LUCA NOVEL

MAGGIE
SHAYNE

NEW YORK TIMES BESTSELLING AUTHOR

OLIVERHEBERBOOKS

Published by Oliver-Heber Books

0 9 8 7 6 5 4 3 2 1

 Created with Vellum

This novel is dedicated to Niblet, the most wonderful little bulldog there ever was. She was my constant sidekick for almost 14 years, the entire existence of the Brown and de Luca series, and she was the inspiration for Myrtle, Rachel's blind bulldog throughout the series. Niblet was not blind. She was a thriving, healthy girl for her entire life right up until the end. She loved food more than air, and she loved snow almost as much as food. And I miss her deeply. This one's for you, Nibs.

CHAPTER 1

10 YEARS AGO

Eva went to The Sapphire Club to rehearse because the new routine wasn't quite there yet. God, she loved the pool room when no one else was around. Chlorine in every breath and echoes of every step. The pool was open, its mechanized cover pulled back into itself. She slid out of her jeans, already wearing her smooth, shiny leggings underneath. Blue, not that it mattered. She took off her blouse. Under it, she wore a bikini top with seashell cups. It was padded though, and not as uncomfortable as it looked.

She unzipped her custom garment bag and laid her beautiful mermaid tail out on the cool concrete floor. It was the softest powder blue color at the waist, and then it darkened through every imaginable shade of blue all the way to the rich, deep, midnight color at the wide, fluted tail fin. It was textured like a real fish, with each scale and the edges of the tail highlighted in silver. Its lighter colors were iridescent and shimmered when she moved in the lights. She knew just how to turn, how to swirl, how to flip, to make the costume sparkle and shimmer for the audience.

She put the end of a long-handled hook through her zipper pull and laid it where she'd be able to reach it, and then she wriggled into the tail, toes first, lying on her belly. She took hold of the wood handle of the hook to pull up the zipper. Her tail was skin-tight, and it took both arms and risked dislocated shoulders to do it by herself.

Most of the mermaids couldn't do it without help, but Eva had been at this awhile and her Paul had spent more than he probably should have on a this one. A wedding gift, he'd said. Custom made with a newfangled easy-zip design.

"Easy, my tail," she said, but she was smiling when she dropped the zipper pull and rolled onto her back. She flipped her tail and admired its delicate patterns. Every crease held hidden silver that winked and shone in the light. It was the most beautiful tail she'd ever seen. She loved her tail.

Paul had designed it himself, even though latex wasn't his medium. He was a metal sculptor, her new husband. He made whimsical creatures and plants out of steel, and sold enough to make a comfortable living.

He'd created the tail's design, then found someone with the skill to make it. He knew a lot of artists and sculptors. He said the colors were perfect with her long, raven curls. That's what he called them, long raven curls.

He was a kind and wonderful man.

It *wasn't* a mistake, marrying him. He was everything

good and she was determined to love him the way he loved her. And she could, she knew she could.

He *adored* her. Had fallen for her the first time he'd seen her in this very pool, he'd said, when some friends had dragged him to The Sapphire Club for a show. Normally, he was a homebody. But after that night, he had come to every performance— like a freaking stalker, Hannah had said, but it wasn't like that. She'd had one "fan" who'd given her that kind of vibe. She knew what that felt like. They'd stopped coming to shows though. Maybe now that she was married, they'd given up.

Eventually, Paul had managed to find an opening to introduce himself.

Eva rolled to the edge of the water and right over into the dark pool. Cool water engulfed her and she let herself sink, then executed a graceful spiral, and with a flip of her tail, swam deeper. From the bottom, she looked out the front of the tank. This aquarium was special; tempered glass, not acrylic. Not many tanks still were, but the owners had been adamant. Had it custom made with a spare front pane, in case they stopped making them entirely.

They were like that, the three owners of The Sapphire Club. The billionaire bad boys, everyone called them. Personally, she thought they were spoiled, entitled jerks with a shared mermaid fetish.

They paid well, though, and the big twice-a-year bonuses were worth the occasional blatant ogling. She bet some of the team got a little more, maybe gave a little more, too. But she wasn't one to judge.

Through the thick, clear glass, she could see the club's

main room. It was dark, like the pool. All the chairs were up on top of all the tables. The hardwood bar was along the left side, from her perspective. Its surface gleamed. The club's cocky head bartender was a bear about his bar. She'd set down a glass without a coaster one night and he'd leaned right up in her face, yelling at her. She actually thought he might hit her.

She did not like that guy, and it was mutual. She'd left an empty glass on the bar three nights in a row now, and he had to know it was her. Screw him. She was gonna do it again tonight.

She pushed Earl Mackey out of her mind and executed a few warmup moves. Using her tail had become second nature to Eva after seven seasons as Mermaid Esmeralda at The Sapphire Club. She loved this gig. She loved everyone here other than Mackey and the owners. She especially loved the other performers. They were like a family. They had even attended her wedding.

She gazed at the brand-new rings on her left hand as she stopped near an underwater lily with a concealed air hose for a couple of breaths. And then a ripple of alarm went through her because she'd forgotten to take her rings off, and she didn't know if chlorinated water would hurt them.

Too late now.

She got nicely oxygenated, then swam off behind the boulder and fake seaweed to begin her routine. She tapped her underwater headphones, and the music came up, Enya's "Adiemus." The song's lyrics were made-up, not a real language. So they could mean anything she wanted.

Eva had decided they told the story of a woman who

found the world above too cruel and complicated to bear, and who wanted to be a mermaid for real, instead of just make believe. A reverse fairy tale.

Wouldn't that be something?

She wouldn't even need the ocean. Saratoga Lake was just beyond the back parking lot. The club offered shoreline wedding packages, complete with Eva and her pals in Mermaid Pose on those boulders along the shoreline.

The song for Eva's routine would be playing on speakers for the first show of the season tomorrow, but she needed to be able to hear it, too, to get her moves synched perfectly to the beat. She wouldn't be able to wear the headphones during the show, so she had to practice over and over.

The music started. On the third beat, she swam out and across the back of the pool, offering the audience a tantalizing glimpse where the soft, rippling light barely reached. That was when all the chattering diners would go silent, not that she could hear them in the pool, but she'd seen video from out there. That first glimpse always got their attention.

Behind the boulder on the opposite side, she got another breath, then swam out again, closer to the font this time. She paused in the middle to gaze, wide-eyed, at the non-existent diners, then darted into hiding again. After a beat, she peeked out from behind the plastic shipwreck, then ducked behind it again. Another breath, and then she swam right up to the glass and waved hello.

In the actual show, a performer with a shark tail and dorsal fin would show up to chase her around a few times, and that was when she got to execute her best moves.

As the music swelled, she imagined Hannah in her shark

costume coming at her, gave a burst of speed, and executed a triple spiral to evade. The plan was, they'd both dart behind rocks for a breath, then come out again, and twine around each other in mock combat. She did the moves on her own, then went for another breath, but there was no air coming out of the lily hose.

That was weird.

She swam across to the other side of the tank, feeling a strange vibration as she did. But she was more concerned with getting a breath. The air-lily on that side was still working, so she got a few breaths as she went over the next moves in her head. The way they had to twist around each other without touching, and then as they parted, they would somersault in opposite directions, perfectly synchronized.

The music was swelling now, she'd have to skip the tangle and go straight to the rolls to keep time. So she swam out and rolled once forward, then once backward, then once forward and once more back, creating a lemniscate in the water.

It was on the second backward roll that she noticed the surface of the dark pool looked odd and, in a flash, realized the floor over the pool was in motion. It was closing, pushing water before it. It was nearly closed!

With a powerful flip of her tail, she propelled herself upward, toward the rapidly closing gap, and then she couldn't stop her momentum and bashed her head into the barrier as it closed all the way.

She yelped, and released a bubble of sound that went nowhere. Her heart was pounding as she pressed her hands to the underside of the floor. There was no space between it and the water— no air pocket.

She had to let someone know she was in the pool!

She swam to the front and banged on the glass with fists but saw no sign of anyone out there. Then she went back to the air-lily behind the rock, the one that still worked.

Only it wasn't working anymore.

Nor did any of the other hidden air-supply hoses.

Again, she surged to the front, pounding the aquarium glass with her fists. It occurred to her, as her lungs began to spasm and she held her nose to keep from sucking in water, that someone must have done this. Someone must have closed the floor and turned off the air supply.

Someone...

Her lungs spasmed hard. Water rushed in and it felt like relief. It felt cool and soothing as her final thought completed itself.

Someone had killed her.

MISTY

Zig handed Misty a five-by-seven black-and-white photo she'd probably printed for dramatic effect. "Eva Quaid, vanished without a trace ten years ago," she said. "She was a twenty-seven-year-old newlywed who waited tables for a living and performed as a professional mermaid on the side."

"She was a mermaid?" Misty's interest was caught, as Zig

had probably known it would be. They'd shared a dorm room last year too, so they knew each other pretty well. Misty knew that Zig's real name was Karen Ziglar, which she hated because *Karen*. She also knew that Zig hated her braces and loved her corn rows.

She looked at the photo. She'd seen this woman before. "Where did she work?"

"Same place you do. The Sapphire Club."

Misty frowned as Zig went on. "One night she left her woodland log cabin home and her brand-new husband Paul, and she never came back. Her car was found abandoned at a rest area off Eighty-Seven, twenty miles north of Saratoga Springs, not far from where she lived. But Eva Quaid was never seen again."

"She worked at The Sapphire Club?"

Zig nodded. "Yes. Did you hear the rest, or have you been—"

"I heard. I'm interested. Go on."

That elicited a look of relief or something. Wait a minute, what was Zig up to? "She was declared legally dead three years ago, but nobody knows what really happened to her. This is the story I want to do for season two of *Zig-Tales*," she said. She took back the photo, crossed the dorm room, and pinned it to a bulletin board, dead center. "'The Mystery of the Missing Mermaid.' I want to re-open that ice-cold case. Better yet, I want to *solve* it." She adjusted the oval wire-rimmed glasses that were too small for her face. "But I only want to do it if you'll help me," she said.

Misty didn't answer right away. "You want me to help you?"

"That's what I said, yeah."

"Well... I um..." Something was going on here. Misty's chest felt all pattery, like she'd just run up a flight of stairs. "I can't really do a podcast about my side job," she said. "Nobody knows about it. I mean, Christy knows I work at a club out here, but she assumes I wait tables or tend bar. I haven't told any of them anything specific."

Zig put down her notebook and looked her in the eye. "Why the hell not? You're *amazing* at it."

"I don't know, it just seems... kind of silly. Like performing as a Disney princess."

"Don't disrespect those girls. Sun pounding down, standing on concrete all day, putting up with pissy, germy whiny-ass kids and smiling the whole time? You couldn't *pay* me enough."

"You're right."

"Besides, I don't need you on the air. I'm the talent."

"Gee, thanks."

"You're my insider, Misty. I want you to partner with me on this."

"Partner?"

"I'll even change the name of the show if you want. I think we'd be dynamite as a team. Though, you're right, you shouldn't go public until the end of this season. You know, it'd blow your cover."

"Right."

"And then only if you want to. It's up to you. But I need you." Zig put her hands on Misty's shoulders. "Besides, it's for a fellow mermaid. She needs you, too."

"You don't take no for an answer, do you?" Misty said it with a smile, because she didn't like confrontation.

"Oh, come on. You're as interested as I am. I can see it in your face."

It was true, she'd been instantly engrossed. And she *did* have experience with crime solving. Her aunt was marrying a cop who'd been part of the family since she was sixteen. Her boyfriend was a cop, too. And... she'd been through some shit.

They were in their dorm room, and it was kind of a mess. "I just think you're in the best position to help me. Besides, my first thought when I started digging into this case was whether it's even safe for you to be working there. Or for *anyone* to be. You might be working with a *killer*."

Misty rolled her eyes. "You said it happened ten years ago. No way the killer's still there."

"Ten years ago," she said. "I have a list of everyone who was employed there when she vanished." She grabbed her tablet, tapped and swiped and turned it Misty's way.

Misty frowned at the list.

"Earl Mackey— head bartender," Misty read, looking up and meeting Zig's eyes. "He's the manager now. My boss."

"Yeah. And it was common knowledge he and Eva hated each other's guts."

Misty kept reading. "Barron White, Raphael Jones, Andrew Chay. Those are the owners."

"They were then, too," she said. "Keep reading."

Misty's gaze returned to the list of unfamiliar names, then paused on one she knew. "Hannah Duke— performer. Is that *Coach* Hannah?"

"The one and only. Still there after ten years."

"So, she knew Eva."

"They all knew Eva."

"Yeah, but I don't think any of them could've— I mean they must've been investigated and cleared, right?"

Zig shrugged. "What I wouldn't give to see the police file."

"Well, did you ask?"

"They're not gonna give it to me just because I ask, Misty."

"Sometimes they have to. You ever hear of the Freedom of Information Act?"

"FOIA." She said it like kids said "Duh." "See? That's why I need you," she said. "And the timing, with the tenth anniversary coming up, it couldn't be better. I have the introductory episode ready to go, but I want you to look at the script. You're a better writer than I am."

Aunt Rachel would say it was in her blood. Her *fucking* blood, Misty corrected inside her own head. Zig was passionate about this. Hell, Misty thought she knew Zig pretty well and she'd never seen her this passionate about anything.

And she was good at what she did. Her little one-woman podcast had uncovered a dognapping ring last fall. A handful of losers had been working the dog parks in wealthy neighborhoods, snatching pedigreed pooches, then re-selling them. Several prominent Saratoga Springs women got their best friends back thanks to Zig's investigation, and their gratitude had paid a whole semester's tuition, which was saying something.

"I have two sponsors this season, did I tell you?"

"Several times," Misty said.

"So, I can pay you to help me."

That got Misty's attention. "How much?"

"Fifteen percent of the take."

"Define take."

Zig lifted her brows. "You sure you're not pre-law? Whatever the sponsors pay me, I'll give you fifteen percent."

"That's meaningless if I don't know what they're paying you."

"It's impossible to say, it depends on the hits and clicks and shit. What do you want, a fucking prospectus?"

"Thirty percent. And I'll help you get those hits and clicks up."

She crooked one eyebrow. "You're an environmental science major."

"I've been helping my aunt with her social for years."

"Who's your aunt?"

It had never come up. Misty didn't bring it up because it would've felt too braggy.

"Rachel de Luca." She nodded at the phone in Zig's hand as she said it.

Zig tapped her thumbs so fast they blurred, then went, "Whoa. Okay, thirty percent. You do our social and help with the investigation. You uh— have any experience with crimes and investigations?"

"A little." She extended her free hand and Zig shook.

And that was how it started.

RACHEL

If the bullshit I wrote about was true— and I'd pretty much decided it was— then I wouldn't be drowning.

My eyes were squeezed tight, but I forced myself to open them, to try to see my underwater world. Something was waving in the darkness— sea grasses, I realized, and there were oversized flowers so big they looked fake. They were fake! The sides of my world were smooth and made of glass, but it was even darker beyond them, and I could see my reflection.

I was not me; I had long, curly hair, darker than my own chestnut brown, and sparkles on my cheeks. I wore a clam-shell bra, and I had a long, gorgeous tail, covered in scales of iridescent blue— lighter at the top and darker at the tail. I tried to move it, and the tail swept through the water, star-tling me so much I almost gasped. I *wanted* to gasp, I realized.

I *had to* gasp.

I needed air. I had to breathe!

I flexed everything from my abs to my toes, and my powerful tail propelled me upward through the water. I expected to burst through the surface and drag in a big breath of air. Instead, my head smashed into something solid and pain shot down my spine. The dancing sea grasses made stripes of light and shadow as I sank through them to the bottom.

Then I lay there on my back and opened my eyes for what

I feared would be the last last time. But I was in my own warm bed, beside my sexy cop. He was tipped up on his side, looking at me. My little bulldog lay across my feet, snoring like a chainsaw.

"What?" I asked.

"You were twisting, sort of. Seemed agitated. I was debating whether to wake you, but Myrtle flopped across your legs and you got peaceful."

I sat up, shaking off the weirdest dream I'd ever had. Then I wiggled my toes to make sure they were still there, because looking under the covers would've been too obvious. I was not about to admit to my guy that I'd dreamed I was a mermaid. That would blow my hard-ass image right out of the water, pun intended.

"You should probably not wake me from a dream unless it looks dire," I told him. "In case it's, you know, one of *those* dreams." Because if it was one of *those* dreams, I needed to experience every detail I could get. *Those* dreams came for a reason. They were, it turned out, work assignments. You know, for my side gig "consulting" with the cops.

"It looked pretty dire for a second there."

I glanced down at his sexy chest and asked myself why I was in such a hurry to get out of bed.

It's not too late, Inner Bitch suggested. *Lay the fuck back down.*

"You want to tell me about the dream?" he asked. "Another nightmare about the wedding?"

"No, hon, nothing like that."

There was only just the one, Inner Bitch reminded me.

Yeah, one in which I kissed my new husband on the shore

14

of the reservoir where we lived, then turned smiling to find our family all gazing, horrified, past us. My sister screamed and pointed, so I turned to look.

There were Misty and Christy, my beautiful twin nieces, lying dead in the shallows, their faces in the shell-shards and sand, their hair moving with the waves.

To a person whose dreams sometimes came true, that one was traumatic.

They don't come true. The ones that do, aren't dreams at all. More like you do a ride-along inside some killer's mind, Inner Bitch said. *Or a mermaid's. The one about the twins was just a stress dream. Marry the man, already.*

While my wedding nightmare was unlike those other kinds of dreams, it might still portend doom. Maybe all the death was symbolic, rather than literal. But what could a pair of dead nieces symbolize, besides disaster?

I hadn't told Mason any of the details of the dead twins dream. He knew I'd had a nightmare about the wedding but thought I couldn't remember details. I had to tell him that much. He'd known something was wrong.

"Rache?" Mason prompted.

I pulled my feet out from under Myrtle and she growled in her sleep. "It was a what-the-hell-did-I-eat-before-bed kind of dream," I said. Then I frowned, trying to recall. "What did I eat last night?"

"The surf-n-turf at Aiello's."

"Well, that explains it, then. Too rich and too delicious. There had to be a downside. I'm good. I'm good."

He lifted his brows, but he hadn't sat up yet. Inner Bitch was right, I needed to get back in. I slid myself lower and my phone rang. I glanced at it, and then turned it to show Mason.

He made a pouty lip and flung back the covers. Then he walked naked to the bathroom while I admired the dimples in his perfect ass. The phone had stopped ringing by the time the bathroom door closed behind him, so I had to call my sister back.

Sandra picked up on the first ring and didn't say hello. "Sorry if I woke you," she said. "I didn't realize how early it was until it was too late."

"I was awake." I slid out of bed and pulled on a light cotton bathrobe. It was pink, the color as soft as the fabric. I loved the way it felt against my skin, especially in the summertime. "Just got up, actually. About to get some coffee. I finally figured out the timer on the new pot, and if the smell tickling my nostrils is anything to go by, it worked."

"I'm coming over," she said. "I have some things to show you."

I didn't need to ask what kinds of things. Wedding things. She was as eager to get us wed as Mason was. I had been, too, up until that dream. Damn dream.

"I haven't showered yet," I said. "Give me an hour. And bring donuts."

"When do I not bring donuts?"

I grinned and disconnected.

Myrtle was still sawing logs, and probably wouldn't wake for another half hour. I heard the shower turn on. When we'd rebuilt after the fire five years ago, we'd done it right. Heated tiles, jacuzzi bathtub, and multiple shower heads.

The most inviting shower in the world, currently occupied by the sexiest guy you know.

"When you're right, you're right, Inner Bitch." I decided my coffee could wait just a little bit longer, shed the robe, and went to join Mason in the shower.

CHAPTER 2

I hugged Mason for a little longer than usual at the door and found the bulge of his sidearm comforting. I didn't feel right. Something was up.

My sister's EV had slipped in, silent as a ninja. She was already steps from the front door. Sandra was younger than me physically, older in every other way. Her hair was currently multiple shades of blond and curved inward at mid-neck. She wore white capri clam-diggers, strappy gold sandals, and a baggy T-shirt that said "Not today, Satan" on the front. A big straw shoulder bag with a hot-pink Shasta daisy woven into it hung heavy from her shoulder. The thing was large enough to hold her worldly possessions. "Get a room," she called, while I kissed my man goodbye.

He grinned at me, and I rolled my eyes, then he said, "Have a great day," and headed down the driveway.

When he passed Sandra, he leaned in and muttered something, then he headed to the Beast, a restored, black '74

Monte Carlo, and got in. When he started it, I could feel its rumble in my chest.

Sandra stepped into my line of sight, then, to hug hello while Mason drove over our long, narrow dirt road back toward the relative civilization of Whitney Point, NY, "Best by a dam site!" Seriously, that was our town motto, because there was a dam, which created the reservoir I saw whenever I looked or stepped outside my house.

If you have to explain it, Inner Bitch began.

"Hey, Sis, it's a gorgeous morning," I said. "Let's take your wedding brochures down to the dock, okay?"

"You don't know that's why I'm here."

"Don't I?" I nodded at the three-ring binder I could see through the top of her gaping, overstuffed bag. "Don't I, though?"

She rolled her eyes and pivoted toward the dock. "There are homemade donuts in here too, so—"

"I'll be right out with the coffee." I leaned down and scratched Myrt's head. "Wanna go look for froggies?"

"Yarf," she replied, and bounded out the front door on her own.

"Sandra!" I was so startled by Myrt's behavior I sort of barked too.

Sandra crouched down to intercept my runaway bulldog. "Well, what's set you on fire today, Myrt? Come on, I'm right here, come to Aunt Sandra."

My dog wiggled her way to my sister, who scratched her head and said, "I've got her."

"Okay." I ran back in for our coffees, and minutes later we were sitting in Adirondack chairs with thick cushions, big footrests, and wide arms to hold our snacks. Myrtle was upright and alert in between us, because she might be blind, but my bulldog had a nose like a bloodhound. And my sister's homemade donuts were one of her favorite smells.

I ate a bite and fed one to my dog, as one does. "Ohmygod, that's fucking amazing." I did not say the words voluntarily.

She took a long, slender box with a tiny pink bow on it from her bag and handed it to me.

"It's like you're bribing me with this shit. Donuts *and* a present?"

"Maybe I am."

I gave the box a little shake. "It's heavy. You don't need to bribe me to plan my own wedding, you know."

"You can drag your feet all you want on your own wedding," she said.

"I'm not dragging my—"

"I need your help with something else. And it's not that big a bribe, just a little thing I saw online. I got the girls each one. Gave it to them their last visit home. Of course, instead of thank-yous, I got eye-rolls, but whatever."

"They're brats. In your twenties, you think you know everything. I promise I will not roll my eyes." I took the lid off the box and stared in at a two-and-a-half-inch long, tacky metal mermaid.

A fucking mermaid. Like in my dream.

Inner bitch hummed the X-Files theme inside my head. Myrtle looked up at me, like she could feel the ice-water chill that danced up my spine.

"Isn't it cute?" Sandra took the thing from its box before I could.

"It's adorable," I said. "What the fuck is it?"

"It's a Crisis Companion."

"Well, obviously." I might've been too heavy on the sarcasm. Then I read the flyer—A young woman's best friend in the cold, cruel world.

Not sarcastic enough, Inner Bitch said.

It was stainless steel. Sandra started unfolding things from the mermaid like it was one of those Boy Scout knives. "This is a rape whistle. This one will cut right through a seat-belt. See? That's a razor blade in the crevice." I nodded so she'd move the thing back out of my face. "This one will break the windshield glass, you know, if your car goes in the water and you can't get out. You just hold it up to the glass, push this button, and..."

She pushed the button and a little metal bolt popped anticlimactically out the end. She pushed it back in with a click. "And this one's a tire pressure gauge. And this one's—"

"That's really thoughtful, Sis. I'm going to keep this in my car at all times."

Yeah, in the glove compartment. Out of sight.

"No need. It comes with a chain, so you can wear it like a necklace. That way you'll always have it if you need it. And it will make me feel better knowing you have it, because I love you and I never want anything bad to happen to you."

I heard the unspoken "again" behind her words, but to her credit she didn't say it aloud. And honestly, for the past couple of years it seemed our energy had shifted. Nothing awful had happened in—

Don't jinx it! Inner Bitch screamed in my head, but I felt to my toes that it was already too late.

I pulled off the pendant I was wearing, an iridescent opal, and tucked it deep into my jeans pocket. Then I draped my sister's offering around my neck.

I leaned over my chair to hug her. "Thank you. It's the most practical, thoughtful, loving gift ever, and I will cherish it."

But why a mermaid? Inner Bitch asked.

"What made you pick a mermaid?" I echoed.

She shrugged. "I don't know. It spoke to me."

"What did it say?"

She frowned as if I'd lost my mind, so I laughed it off.

We ate our donuts and sipped our coffee while it was still hot. The sun was bright on the water, frosting every ripple in neon white and flashing in our eyes every now and then.

Eventually, she said, "I'm a little worried about you. Covid is over. All the reasons to delay the wedding are gone. And yet, you don't seem very interested in getting it planned."

I'd closed my eyes a few words in so I could feel her. She was deflecting.

"That's not what's bothering you," I said. And then, "God, these are good," as I finished the last bite of donut and wondered how bad it would be to have a second. But back to my sister. "Christy told me that you've been over-protective lately. And that rape whistle, survivalist do-all-tool—"

"Crisis Companion," she corrected.

"—seems to support her claim. What gives?" Because I'd dreamt about my nieces being dead, and my sister was having over-protective mother's intuition vibes. Something was definitely up.

Sandra sighed and gave Myrtle the rest of her half-eaten donut. "I don't know. I don't know. Since they moved out on their own, I just worry all the time."

"I bet that's normal," I told her. "They're away from home in a way that feels permanent." Misty was in her sophomore year and living on campus at Skidmore, two and a half hours away by car. My sister acted like she'd moved across the country. Christy had a job in retail, an apartment in nearby Binghamton, and was taking online classes in whatever struck her interest. Sandra wasn't thrilled about those choices, either.

"I don't know if that's it, but I do know that Misty's keeping secrets."

"How do you know that?" Screw it. I ate another donut, gave a tiny piece to Myrtle, then I said, "All gone," and brushed my hands together so she could hear it.

"She's never home," Sandra said. "She's always distracted. She's refusing calls all the time. I mean, she usually texts me back after a little while. She's barely coming home anymore, not even on weekends."

Myrtle sighed as if heartbroken and wandered off the dock and down to the edge of the water for a drink. It was unusual for her to get far from my side. I did not like this independent streak.

"Well the semester's winding down," I said. "She's probably in transition."

"No, this is more. She's distracted all the time."

"I'm sure she's made friends out there. She's a sopho-more, she must have."

"Look, I'm telling you, something is wrong. All my mommy-alarms are vibrating. I feel this, Rachel, I feel it clearly. You work with Mason on cases all the time," she said. "You know how to—"

"Snoop?" I asked. I made my eyes really wide. "Are you seri-ously asking me to spy on your grown-ass daughter, Sandra?"

She smacked her palm on the wide, flat arm of her chair and said, "Yes! That's *exactly* what I'm asking, and I know I sound crazy, but you are my sister, and you have to do this for me, because I'm going to go insane if I don't know for sure she's okay."

That logic isn't logical.

No, but it was effective. "Of course I will, I'll... I'll drive out for a visit for starters, huh? See if she'll open up to her Auntie Badass before we resort to pawing through her dorm-room trash, okay?"

Sandra's brows went soft. "Really? Will you? God, I'd feel so much better, Rache."

"I will. Hell, maybe a weekend in Saratoga Springs is just the ticket. Mason's been acting a little mopey lately."

"Do you blame him?"

I had taken a sip of my now-cold coffee and choked on a chunk of soggy donut. "What's that supposed to mean?" And then I remembered and went on. "And what was that little exchange between you two when you passed on the sidewalk this morning?"

"What exchange?"

I looked down at my cold, donut-polluted coffee so I could feel her, not that I thought she'd lie to me, but still. And then I got stuck looking because of the patterns in the dark, crumby liquid.

How weird, it almost looked like something was swimming around in—

A fishtail rose so hard it splashed coffee into my face. "Holy shit!" I jumped up fast and pressed my hands to my cheeks but there was no coffee wetting my skin. Not a drop stained my light denim jacket, either. And the mug on the arm of my chair was still, not even a ripple in its shiny black surface.

"What the hell, Rachel?"

"I don't fucking know!" My voice came out too loud, too sharp. I took a breath. "Reflection in the mug," I said. "My eyes were playing tricks on me."

Sandra got to her feet and her expression shifted instantly to sheer worry. "Is your eyesight okay? Have you been having issues? Have you talked to your doctor?"

"It's nothing like that."

She searched my face, put one palm on my cheek like a mom checking her kid for a fever. "You'd tell me if something was wrong, wouldn't you?"

"I would. I swear. And honestly, Sandra, my biggest problem right now is..." I looked around my home, but I didn't see any problems to list for her. Honestly, life was about as good as I could imagine it. Jeremy was a six-month rookie deputy at the Broome County Sheriff's Department. Josh had graduated and decided to spend some time traveling across the country with his best buddies and had taken his dog, Hugo, along with him. Mason and I were having a summer of bliss. No kids. No catastrophes. No dead people talking inside my head or sending me on ride-alongs with killers. Nada. It was bliss.

Up to now, Inner Bitch said, the fucking know-it-all.

I glanced down at my dog. She was standing rigid, staring straight down at a shiny green frog, who was also completely motionless.

I tilted my head. "Myrtle?"

She did not move.

"What's she doing?" Sandra asked.

"I don't know. She's a strange little dog."

"Looks like she's staring at the frog."

"Except she's blind," I said. "But she knows it's there. Jeseze, move, Froggy." I found a pebble near my foot and pitched it at the frog. It splashed near enough to startle it, so it leaped away.

I sat back down, reached for my mug, then let my hand glide right on by. No thanks. "That's my only problem right now, Sis. My bulldog is acting oddly."

And you're afraid if you get married your nieces will die, Inner Bitch pointed out. *And you're maybe being haunted by a mermaid.*

There are no such things as mermaids, I thought back at her. This was something else. A brain tumor, maybe.

"You sure you're okay?" Sandra asked.

"Yeah. I'm good. Fine."

"Okay, good. That's settled. So, about your wedding—"

"Actually, let me get on the Misty situation. Because... I

can't focus on the wedding until I make sure my niece is safe."

My sister looked at me the way she looked at her twins when they were lying to her face. "You just said she was probably fine."

"Yeah, but— but I'll feel better when I make sure."

And you don't want to talk about the wedding.

"Is there some reason you don't want to talk about your wedding, Rachel?"

It always gave me a chill when my inner voice agreed with my sister. "Can't it be that I just don't feel like it yet?"

"You've been engaged since before the pandemic."

"And we had to delay the wedding three times during the pandemic. Every time we thought it was over—"

"But now it really is," she said. "Mostly. We have vaccines. Rache, I'm your sister. You can tell me the truth. I'm on your side, you know that, right?"

"Of course I know that."

Sighing, I gazed out at the water and foothills beyond. God, I loved it here. Especially in the fall when the leaves started to turn, but my second favorite season was the spring. The leaves on the trees were all young and new, and every week something else burst into bloom. The poplars, the cherries, the apple trees.

A fish jumped. A mosquito landed on my arm. I smacked and missed.

"Are you and Mason okay?" Sandra asked said at length.

That made me sit up straight, my impending mellow shattered. "Of course we are. We're more than okay. We're sickeningly okay."

Her brows rose, her eyes closed. She blew a sigh through O-shaped lips and said, "Thank goodness. I was getting worried."

"You never have to worry about that."

She smacked her hand on the binder. I think it was louder than she intended. It made me jump. "Then what the hell is the problem?"

Was I going to tell my sister that I'd had a dream her twin daughters were dead, and didn't know if it was a premonition, a warning from the other side, or an impending psychotic break? No. She had enough to worry about, the enough being that her kids had the audacity to grow up and leave her.

"If you guys are okay, and there's nothing wrong," she said, in a slow-build-up kind of way, and then she flipped open the book, "let's at least pick the dress!"

I glanced down. Before my eyes was a stack of catalogues from wedding boutiques, and I had no choice but to look through them with her. I took the one from the top and leaned back in my chair. Sandra did the same, and soon we were leaning over to show each other gowns— she as suggestions, me as punchlines.

When I showed her one with a big bustle and said, "For the bride with no ass of her own," my sister did not laugh. She kind of scowled at me, so I flipped pages with what I hoped was a more serious attitude.

"Honestly, why do wedding gowns all have to look like they belong on aspiring cartoon princesses?"

"What don't you like?" Sandra asked, glancing over to see where I was looking.

"Poofy skirts. Poofy sleeves. Poofy veils.

"So, nothing poofy."

"I want something dignified. I'm not twenty-two."

You are way *not twenty-two.*

Shut up, Inner Bitch.

"Elegant," Sandra said, "but not fussy."

"And a little bit sexy," I added.

"Mm-hmm. Mm-hmm. I think I know what you mean."

I checked on Myrtle while my sister flipped pages. She was lying down near the water's edge and seemed fine.

Then my sister dropped a catalogue into my lap.

The gown on the front cover was a short one with spaghetti straps and a skirt that flared but was not poofy. It was a little too fun for me, but it was heading in the right direction. I started flipping pages in that particular book to humor my sister and stopped suddenly when my eyes got stuck. There was a simple Grecian gown. It draped from the shoulders, clung until it passed the hips, and then its skirt spilled onto the floor.

"Rachel?"

I didn't answer but was instead trying to picture myself in the dress. I thought I might love it.

Sandra got out of her chair and came to stand behind mine. "Oh, wow. Rachel, that would be stunning on you."

"You think?"

"Do you not see the little heart sticker I put on that page?"

I frowned, then dug at the little pink heart with a finger-nail. "I thought it was part of the layout."

"It's not, and I knew that was the catalogue you'd like

best, and I was pretty sure that was the dress. Although if you want to see the other two you'd love, just look for more hearts. Either way, it's perfect. Because this shop," she took the catalogue from me and flipped to its back cover, tapping her finger on the address, "is in Saratoga Springs."

I looked at her. "Where Misty is."

"Yep. And if we go out there on a wedding gown shopping trip, it won't look like we're checking up on her."

"I— I—" *Aye yi yi.* "You're good. Maybe you should be the one helping Mason solve crimes."

"I have enough trouble solving daughters. So, are we on?"

"Fine. We're on. We'll drive out this weekend, okay?"

"Great. Perfect." She gathered up the catalogues and closed the binder around them.

"You planned this," I accused.

"Yes, I did."

"You know me a little too well, Sis."

"Better than anybody," she said. "I'm heading out. Love you."

"Love you." She kissed the top of my head and headed back across to her car in my driveway. I settled into my chair to finish my coffee. The catalogue was still on its arm, its pages riffling in the breeze that came off the reservoir.

Sandra's van crunched over the gravel road until I couldn't hear it anymore. Just off the edge of the dock, the water stirred in a weird way. I got up, moving nearer the railing for a closer look.

A grown-ass woman with a fucking fish tail breached the surface. She looked right at me and swung that tail my way.

Splash! I threw my arms up in front of my face, but the wave hit me full on all the same. I felt the shock of the cold water drenching me. "What in the actual—" I lowered my arms.

I was dry. My clothes, my hair— everything— bone dry. The water in front me was still and not a ripple indicated it hadn't been the entire time.

"What in the ever-loving fuck *is* this?"

I don't know, Outer Bitch. See what I did there? I'm sticking with the you're-being-haunted-by-a-mermaid theory.

I looked out at the water for a few more seconds. Then, with a sigh, I headed back to the house, grabbing both mugs and the catalogue on the way. "There are no such things as mermaids."

Right. Then what do you think it is?

I shrugged. "I need to call Jeremy. He'll know what's up with Misty, if anyone does. Come on, Myrt. Let's go inside."

She bounced to her feet and ran to my side.

CHAPTER 3

MISTY

Episode two was up. Misty had worked on it with Zig so much that she knew it by heart, but she listened anyway as she drove to work.

"The weekend Eva vanished, her new husband Paul was at the Unique Artists' Expo, in Rochester." Zig's voice, when she was recording, took on a deeper, slower, more deliberate tone. And it was evocative, conveying emotion, suspense, tension. She was born to do this, Misty thought, and not for the first time.

But even Zig admitted the writing this year was way better than last. That was because Misty was the one doing it.

"He attends every year. I spoke to a fellow artist who asked not to be named..."

But Misty knew her name: Sarah Malone. She was a painter from Rochester, one of the event's organizers, and she'd known Paul Quaid since the expo had begun in 2010. Misty and Zig had spent more than an hour talking to her about Quaid, without learning a helluva lot. She described him as a quiet guy, kind of shy. He rarely stayed long at the expo's nightly mixers. UA was his only carved-in-stone annual event, she said, although he would do others, reluctantly, if money was tight. But mostly he sold his work online and that was how he liked it.

"A real loner," Misty murmured to her Jeep. "Aren't they always?"

"Quaid always drives out to Rochester and back in his old Volvo, a trip that takes three hours and twenty-one minutes, according to the internet," Zig was saying in her dulcet but deadly serious podcaster voice. "He always stays in the same hotel room, always orders the same meals. The year his new bride vanished was no different. According to the local press back then, there was enough video footage of Quaid at the event to rule him out as a suspect.

"My silent partner and I were able to find extensive photos and footage of that year's expo online, and we spotted him in several shots. But I don't think the police did what we did. We found, in the local press, the photo with the latest time stamp, a grainy shot of him getting ice from the machine on his floor around midnight on the morning Eva vanished. Witnesses saw Paul Quaid at the breakfast buffet the next morning, according to reporting in the *Springs Herald*, and since the buffet only ran from 6:30 to 7:30 a.m., this provided his alibi. Police Detective Jen Scott, a former Army Explosives Ordinance Specialist, took charge of the case, and she cleared Quaid based on this alibi. But

Detective Scott didn't do what my silent partner and I did either."

Misty smiled to herself. It had been her idea to stand in the spot with the ice maker, turn on a timer, and see how long it took to get back to Saratoga Springs. Driving fast, they'd made it in three hours and two minutes. Making a round trip of—

"Six hours, four minutes," Zig said slowly, drawing out the suspense. "Figure in a half hour to make Eva disappear, and he could still have made it back in time for that breakfast buffet. It would've been tight, but it was entirely possible. This makes us wonder if any of the other suspects the police ruled out have equally shoddy alibis. And we plan to test every single one of them."

There was a two-beat pause, and then, "Don't miss our next episode. Hit that 'Subscribe' button to get notified when it goes live. Thanks for riding along. Peace out."

Misty was always amused when Zig flashed a two-finger peace sign with her sign-off. It was a podcast, audio-only. No video. Nobody could see her, but she always did it.

She pulled in along the driveway that hugged The Sapphire Club. It was a gorgeous place, fire-treated barn boards on the outside, dark brown, even black here and there. The border around the building was a sea-themed rock garden, with boulders, seashells, and sand. The entry doors were red, double, and bracketed by stained-glass sidelights depicting graceful mermaids.

The driveway curved in close for drop-offs, then curved the other way, around to the parking lot in back. The parking lot was paved in blacktop and surrounded by boulders that needed a little more imagination, in her opinion. They just sat there like they'd been dropped. They should have plants and smaller rocks and things around them, to make them seem more natural.

Just past the parking lot and down a little knoll, Saratoga Lake sparkled like a giant sapphire. The Sapphire Club's property extended all the way to the beach. They offered wedding packages all summer long. Lakeshore ceremonies, with or without mermaids posing on rocks for photos. Receptions were held in the club a few yards away, with optional mermaid performances.

They booked out two years in advance. Misty had made serious bank doing those gigs last summer.

She parked her Jeep, headed up the clanging metal staircase to the second-floor entrance, and walked into warm chlorinated humidity. The cover was open, and the pool was blue and inviting. Its lights were on. Echo and Jasmine were already in the water. They did this bit where they made a living mermaid yin-yang symbol. Echo's skin was dark as ebony, and her long dark braids trailed behind her when she swam. Her lashes were so thick she looked like she wore makeup, even when she didn't, and her eyes were big, brown, and full of her feelings. Jasmine was milky pale, right to her eyelashes. Her brows were the same strawberry blond as her long, ultra-fine hair, that looked like smoke when it trailed behind her in the water. Her eyes were ice-blue and revealed nothing.

"Hey girls. Hey, Toby," Misty said, hurling her garment bag from her shoulder to the floor. Toby was face-down on the floor, reaching behind him with a long-handled zipper hook to try to zip his own flaming tail. It had stripes of bright orange, vivid yellow, and blaze red. He'd dyed his hair to match, and it stood up on his head with waterproof mouse.

"Hey, put that hook down before you stab yourself," Misty said, heading over to him and taking the position, straddling his head.

Toby sighed in relief and put the zipper hook down. She reached for the long string that was threaded through his zipper and pulled. She had to lean back to pull it up all the way. Mermaid tails were tight anyway, and Toby's was getting a *little* tighter.

Coach Hannah came in from the locker room door on the right wall, still in the process of bundling up her long, short blond layers. She wore a black spandex tank top and calf-length swim pants, and carried a heavy rubber band that was not for her hair. It was for her legs.

"I have news," she said, and everyone came to attention, including Toby, who was still lying face-down, but propped his chin on his elbows. "The owners are coming."

"When?" Jasmine asked. Her voice was an octave higher than normal. No doubt she planned to show off for them, maybe even land one of them. While her face revealed nothing, her voice was the gateway to her feelings.

"Two weeks," Coach replied.

The owners were three very wealthy men, thanks to their fathers, who'd bought them this place. The Sapphire Club was their fun little hobby. They came out a couple of times every summer and got hammered in the private dining room directly below the locker room on the right side of the pool. The right side of the aquarium formed one wall of the private dining room, so the billionaire bad boys could get a private show. She didn't know why anyone called them "boys." They had to be pushing fast toward forty.

Misty put on her tail as she contemplated yet another visit from the owners. It meant hard work and some squirminess. They always flirted outrageously with the wait staff and the performers. *Especially* the performers. They didn't outright proposition anyone, at least not that Misty had heard. But they let every mermaid there know they would like to have sex.

It was harassment, yes, but who was going to turn them in or complain? It wasn't as if the world was awash in open positions for professional mermaids. Without this gig, you'd either have to move to another city with a tank or make a living doing birthday parties.

Misty really didn't look at this gig as a life goal. It was just a fun side job that she'd fallen in love with. It wouldn't be her career. She hadn't decided what her career would be, but she knew it wouldn't be performing as a mermaid.

She rolled onto her belly. Toby sat up, scooted over, and tugged her zipper up.

"Oooooh baby. Bonus time," Echo said. She leaned up on the edge over the pool's mechanical opening-closing cover and slapped the water with her tail to punctuate her joy.

"We have to do something amazing this time," Toby put in.

The owners always expected a high caliber performance, and they gave the performers big, fat bonus checks every single time. The better the show, the bigger the bonus.

"I have some ideas and I want to hear yours." Coach

Hannah walked over to the pool's edge and pulled the big rubber band on over her feet, up to mid-calf. Then she dove in, her legs locked together, just like a mermaid.

She used the rubber band method for training, but she still had her old tail. It was a real stunner, silver and white and it glittered when any light source hit it. She didn't perform anymore, and Misty thought it was a crying shame. She was good.

Toby had barrel-rolled himself to the edge, and right over the side, leaving Misty the rotten egg. Last one in bought drinks after practice. Shoot.

She crawled on her arms, dragging her tail behind her, slid headfirst into the cool, chlorinated water, and tried not to think about the fact that she was going to slide just as smoothly into Mr. Mackey's office later to search his computer for anything about Eva Quaid.

The club's manager had a temper like a wounded bear, so she'd better not get caught. But he'd been tending bar during the same time Eva had worked there, and the paper had printed a co-worker's opinion that the two had hated each other, so he was a suspect. If nothing else, she should at least be able to pull up Eva's employee files.

She was a nervous wreck. It seemed really bad, breaking the law when her boyfriend was a cop. It kind of seemed like being unfaithful.

She did a few laps around the tank, then surfaced when Coach pointed up. "Warmups," she called as the four merfolk bobbed in the water. "Mermaid Pose! Go!"

They swam to the edge, braced their palms on the floor, and pushed their upper bodies up out of the water, simultaneously arching their backs and throwing back their heads. Misty arched her entire spine and neck, flipping her long, wet hair behind her. This was the iconic Mermaid Pose, and one of most popular photo ops for fans, when struck on the boulders along the lakeshore.

The merfolk lowered into the water, then sprang up into Mermaid Pose again for thirty reps. It was how they began every practice session.

RACHEL

"What makes you think anything's wrong with Misty, Aunt Rache?"

I was sitting across from the handsome young police officer I'd helped to raise, a little bit, just at the end there. His mom was still incarcerated in a maximum-security psychiatric facility for killing a bunch of people and trying to cut out my eyes. His father, Mason's brother, had taken his own life. He'd left a note confessing to a pile of murders— a note nobody ever saw besides Mason and me. Was it any wonder the kid had issues with alcohol?

And yet here he was, a cop, clean and sober and dating my niece Misty.

"Aunt Rache?" he prompted, because I'd gotten lost noticing how he'd turned from lanky teenager to broad-shouldered man overnight.

"You can drop the 'aunt' part, if you want."

He tipped his head sideways, frowned, then shook his head. "I don't think I can."

We were having coffee at the breakfast bar in my kitchen. Myrtle was sitting between our stools with her head tipped up and her smooshed nose twitching. Jere handed her down a tiny corner of his muffin, then yelled, "Ouch!" when she took fingers and all. She did not notice, merely swallowed, and resumed the position— head up, nose twitching.

"But back to Misty."

"I don't know. That's the truth," I said. "But her mother's worried, and I promised I'd..." I didn't finish.

"Should I tell her she's being investigated by her psychic aunt?"

"You know better than to use that word."

"Sorry. Her not-fucking-psychic aunt?"

I thinned my lips and speared him with a glare. He just grinned, but then the smile died. "Misty... she's changing, I think. She's been super busy, really distracted, but at the same time... I don't know. Excited. Animated. Her voice is full of energy, higher pitched, and she talks faster, as if—"

"As if she's on drugs?" My eyes went wide.

He let his head fall forward as if his neck had gone liquid. When he looked up again, dead serious, he said, "I think she's happy. And busy with something she'll tell us all about when she's ready. I'm trying not to be all insecure about that, and I think that might be a good thing for you and her mom to try, too."

"Oh." I blinked slowly. I couldn't tell him about the dead twins dream, and the mermaid apparition would just sound crazy to anyone but Mason. Mason had heard my craziest

41

shit and had yet to run screaming. Fucking guy wanted to *marry* me.

Myrtle gave a little bark, and I used the term loosely. With a bulldog it's more like a snuffly sneeze-cough combo, usually accompanied by a fart of equal volume. Jeremy looked at me, brows up. "She never barks."

"It's new. She's developing an independent streak, too." I fed her a blueberry from my muffin. "What do you think it is, keeping Misty so busy, distracted, and happy?"

"I don't know yet. And if you want to know, you should ask her yourself."

"That's exactly what I plan to do when I see her this weekend."

"You're going out there to spy on her?"

"Actually, I'm going to try on wedding dresses in a chi-chi boutique my sister found."

"To spy on her."

"Well, I might say hello while I'm in town."

He sighed, slid off his stool and rose all tall and strong in his uniform. "I have to go, Aunt Rache. But seriously, just talk to Misty directly. Okay?"

"I will. I promise." I got up with my fingers crossed behind my back, walked him to the door, and waved goodbye as he got into the white Chevy Suburban with "SHERIFF" on the side in red, and Broome County underneath. It had two diagonal bars behind the front tire, black and red, with a gold border between. Not a bad ride, for a rookie.

As soon as he was out of sight, I closed the front door, picked up my phone and called Christy. It went straight to voicemail, so I said, "Something is up with your sister. Call me."

MISTY

Misty was sitting at the bar with a diet soda when Mr. Mackey left his office and headed back to the bathroom at the end of the hall that only he was allowed to use. He went in there at about this time every day, and he never came out for at least twenty minutes.

"I left something upstairs in the locker room," she said, sliding off the barstool, not even checking whether Taylor, the bartender, was listening.

He was, it turned out. "Not with my glass, you're not."

"I'll bring it back."

"Nobody ever brings them back." He tapped the gleaming bar surface with a forefinger and his blond side bang fell over his forehead.

It reminded her sharply of Jeremy's hair, before he'd cut it for the police academy. It was growing back now that he was a working cop, but that young-guy look was history.

He'd broken the news as gently as he knew how, which had been something like, "Sorry, hon. But I won't intimidate many criminals with a Bieber bang." She remembered how he'd flipped his hair off his forehead when he'd said it and flashed that sexy smile of his. He had inherited the Brown family dimples.

She'd mourned his hair for a solid week.

Thinking of Jeremy made her heart turn warm and gooey in her chest. Her twin would call her whipped. But she was just in love. It was a challenge, being so far apart, but they were making it work, and college wouldn't be forever.

She tipped up the glass to drain the ice-water-diluted Diet Coke from the bottom and handed the glass to Taylor.

"Thanks." He resumed wiping the already spotless surface with his with his ever-present towel.

Misty rolled her eyes and walked away toward the front of the room where heavy blue velvet stage curtains hid the tank. The big reveal was a real moment for first-timers. To the right of the tank was a hallway lined in doors. The first door led into the private dining room, where one entire wall was the glass side of the aquarium. Farther right, another door led to the stairs up. Mackey's office was the door across from the stairs on the right. The storage room and private bathroom were farther along the hall.

The rest of them had to use the public restrooms on the opposite side. Only Mackey got to use the shabby little private one.

She started to walk away, felt Taylor's eyes were on her, and wished for a distraction. His phone pinged as if she'd willed it to happen. She glanced back once, to see his head down, eyes focused, so she hurried down the hallway, ducked into Mr. Mackey's office, and closed the door behind her. The doorknob made a loud click when she let go of it, and she froze, listening. But there was only silence. Okay. Good.

She took a deep, calming breath, and turned to look

around the room. Mackey had the owners' eight-by-ten headshots on the walls, the kiss-up. There they were, the billionaire bad boys; Barron White, "Bare" to his friends— okay, probably "Bear," but "Bare" was funnier; Raphael Jones, who went by RJ; Andrew Alexander Chay III, who went by Andrew Alexander Chay III.

She guessed Mackey's need to kiss up to the bosses had outweighed his bigotry. He did a good job hiding his racism. But she'd picked up on it in his attitude toward Echo. His homophobia was right out in the open, too. If not for the bosses, there would be no merman. He'd prefer they not exist. The asshole.

Okay, time to get this over with. She went to the desktop, which was still open, and jiggled the mouse to keep it that way. Then she ran a search on Eva Quaid, but nothing came up.

That was odd.

Wait, wait, Eva and Paul had been newlyweds at the time of her disappearance. She backspaced to erase "Quaid" and ran the search again on "Eva." Eva Mendosa came up. There were five files. She quickly wrestled a thumb drive from her jeans pocket and plugged it in, then she dragged the files over and dropped them. It took all of ten seconds, but it felt like much longer. Finally, she popped the thumb drive back into her pocket, and gave another quick look around the office. It was a mess. There were file folders with coffee rings all over his desk, stacks of mail, empty glasses from Taylor's bar. On a shelf behind the desk, there was a bundle of what looked like wall calendars.

She'd heard the story. It went, "We did a calendar one

year." The end. But she'd never heard which year, and she'd never seen one of them. These must be the leftovers, forever preserved in shrink wrap.

She pushed the desk's swivel chair over to the shelf so she could stand on it to reach up, because she had to get a look at them. Maybe Eva was in them. Maybe it was a clue. Maybe she was just damn curious.

So she climbed up and reached, the chair twisted, and she went down right on her ass on the floor. She'd had an instant fear, while falling, that she might crack her head on the desk and die, then the impact forced every bit of air from her lungs.

Shit, she'd hit hard. How loud had it been? Had anyone heard?

Her heart pounded. She pushed her hair up off her face, and there was a photo looking back at her. It was on the inside of the desk, the part your knees aimed at when you sat in the chair, a 3 x 5 snapshot in a clear plastic frame. Misty rolled onto all fours and used her phone's flashlight. It was Eva, looking at the camera and a man who was looking at Eva like you'd look at the last chocolate bar in existence: with a predatory desire.

Wait a minute, that was no man. That was Mackey! He had *not* aged well.

But this shot did not look as if they hated each other. She was smiling and relaxed, and he was looking like he wanted to devour her. And he had this photo where only he could see it. In an office nobody was supposed to enter. Not even the cleaners.

She snapped a photo of the photo, got to her feet, righted

the chair and went to the door. When she opened it, there was a woman standing on the other side with her hand raised in knocking position. Misty damn near jumped out of her skin.

"Gee, sorry, sorry," she said. "Didn't mean to scare you there." She was tall, long-limbed. Her dark hair was twisted up in back, and she had long bangs over huge brown eyes you could fall into, thick lashes, and crow's feet. Late thirties, maybe.

Misty stepped into the hallway, pulling the office door closed behind her. "Um, if you're looking for Mr. Mackey—"

"No, I'm, uh, looking for you. You're Misty, right?"

She realized the woman was a cop. She knew a cop when she saw one. She was dating a cop, and her almost official Uncle Mason was a cop. She knew cops. "I am," she said. "I know you, don't I? I've seen you here before."

"Good memory," she said. "I come in sometimes, yeah." She handed over a card. "Jen Scott, I'm a detective with the Saratoga Springs Police Department."

Cop. She knew it. And she knew the name. This was the cop in charge of Eva's case. "I just poked my head in looking for Mr. Mackey," Misty said. "But he's not—"

"I don't care what you were doing in your boss's office. That's between you and Earl. Listen, you're roommates with Karen Ziglar, yeah?"

"Zig?" Misty asked.

"She's doing that podcast about the missing mermaid. You're helping her with that, aren't you?" It wasn't really a question.

"What do you..." Misty bit her lip. She knew cops. A

comedy routine popped into her head about a cop's little girl going to confession, saying she didn't recall her sins, and asking for an attorney.

She improvised something similar. "I don't know anything about the podcast, beyond that it exists."

"No? You didn't know your roommate was doing a podcast about a woman who worked where you currently work, doing what you currently do?"

"Like I said, I know it exists."

"Seems something like that would've come up in conversation."

"Seems like you should be talking to Zig."

"Oh, I will be. But right now, I'm talking to you."

Misty pulled out her phone, tapped the screen and turned it toward her. Her background was a shot of Jeremy and Uncle Mason, both in their dress uniforms at Jere's graduation from the academy. "So, should I call my uncle the cop, or my boyfriend the cop?"

"I don't care. You and Zig, you're stirring up trouble with this podcast. You know that?"

"No, I don't know that. What kind of trouble?"

"Fifty calls a day to the department, lunatics leaving bullshit on the tip-line, novel-length letters with theories from alien abduction to witness relocation, and the widower asking me why some college kid is working harder on his wife's case than I am."

"Than you, personally?"

"Yeah, me, personally. It was my goddamn case."

Misty already knew that. She and Zig had read every article published about the investigation into Eva Quaid's disappearance. Misty had helped Zig upload images of every piece to the *Zig-Tales* site. Detective Jen Scott had been quoted all over them.

"I don't know anything about the podcast," she said again, because Detective Scott was doing that long, awkward silence thing that could make shit birds sing like canaries. That was an Aunt Rachel quote, right there. "You should talk to Zig."

"You're helping her. That's what you were doing in the boss's office, wasn't it? Snooping for filler for your podcast? Maybe Eva Quaid's employee records, something like that?"

"I popped in to talk to Mr. Mackey. Door was open. I stepped in, saw he wasn't turned around to leave and bumped into you."

"Got you," she said. "And there he is now."

As if Misty hadn't also heard bathroom door swing open or the sound of a still-running air-dryer.

Detective Scott turned. "Hello, Earl."

"Jen. What brings you by?"

She looked at Misty. "Didn't you want him for something?"

"Yeah, um, the locker room's chilly AF. The team's asking if you can turn up the heat."

He looked from one of them to the other as if he knew something was up, but instead of saying more, he moved between them into his office, behind the desk, took a key from the top left drawer, and then brought it out and handed it to Misty. "Here's the key to the control panel. Nobody touches it but Coach Hannah. Bring it back when she's done."

"Thanks. Nice meeting you, Detective Scott."

"I'll be in touch," she said, and then she walked into Mackey's office and closed the door behind her.

Misty knew damn well she'd already pushed her luck too far, but she pushed it further anyway, and pressed her ear up against the door.

"You aware of this mermaid podcast?" Jen Scott asked.

"Oh, I'm aware."

"It's making the department look bad."

"You mean it's making *you* look bad," Mackey said, but in a sympathetic tone.

There was a heavy sigh. "Chief wants closure on this. My ass is on the line."

"Nobody blames you."

There was some shuffling, a footstep or two coming her way. Misty went stiff and looked around for the closest cover in case the door opened again. There wasn't any.

"I blame me," the detective said. "I don't know, I was almost over it, I think and then this podcast thing comes along, and it's in my face again. People calling the station, three angry letters to the editor in the paper. So far. There'll be more. The freaking morning DJ at WSPN was talking about it yesterday."

"The campus station?" Mackey asked. "At least it's smalltime."

"Has this podcast thing hurt your business?"

Misty went stiff, listened harder. Zig had deliberately not mentioned The Sapphire Club by name, but it was the only club in the Springs with a mermaid show. They'd discussed it and decided to err on the side of not getting sued.

"Business... has picked up, actually. People are curious."

"People are sick fucks."

"That they are," Mr. Mackey said. "We've had a coupl'a nasty phone calls, but nothing I can't handle."

"Send me the numbers. It's harassment. I'll pay the assholes a visit."

Mackey laughed softly, like he loved the idea of her intimidating the callers. Then his laugh stopped abruptly. "Jesus, I hope the assholes aren't bothering Paul." Then, "What's that? What's that look? Don't tell me you suspect Paul again, after all this time."

Footsteps came toward the door, and Misty tiptoed backwards up the hall, so if that door opened, she could shift into walking forward. That would work, right?

"You do, don't you?" Mr. Mackey asked. "I thought you cleared him, back then?"

"You know I can't talk about the case, Earl."

"Come on. You seriously think Paul could've *hurt* Eva?"

"I think he *did* hurt Eva," she blurted.

Misty stopped backing up and moved a few steps closer again. If she could have perked her ears, she would have.

"I've *always* thought it," the detective went on slowly. "And if I could get a search warrant for that freaking cabin, I bet I could figure out *how*."

The hair on Misty's arms was standing up straight. Then the doorknob turned, and the office door opened just a little. "And if you tell anyone I said that, I'll find a reason to shut this place down."

"Who'm I gonna tell?" Mackey asked.

Misty backed up two more silent steps, then ducked sideways into the main dining room. By the time Detective Scott came down the hall, she was on a bar stool in front of a fortuitously forgotten glass with a little bit of something dark in the bottom, rum or Coke or both, and a swizzle stick. She grabbed the swizzle and stirred the melting ice cubes around in the liquid.

Behind the bar, Taylor pushed his long blond bang off his forehead and frowned at her.

Detective Scott glanced at her, then at the glass, then her again. She gave a nod, then crossed the dining room and went out the main entry doors, all the way on the opposite end of the room as the stage.

Misty pulled out her phone and texted Zig.

Misty: Need to talk ASAP.

CHAPTER 4

"What? What is it?" Zig asked. She'd met Misty on the busy sidewalk outside their dorm, didn't even wait for her to come in. Her glasses were red-framed today, and the eyes behind them were excited.

Misty took her hand and started back the way she'd come. "Too many people," she said under her breath, tugging her toward the quad. When they were out of earshot of others, she leaned close, talking as fast as she was walking. "Cop came to the club today asking me about your podcast, saying it was stirring up a lot of interest in the case. Says it was her case."

"Detective Scott?" Zig widened her eyes, then paced away. "She probably saw the damn FOIA request for the case files, too. What did you tell her?"

They passed a group of freshmen. You could always tell freshmen because of the fear in their eyes. After they were out of earshot she said, "That I didn't know anything about it. She didn't find that credible, being that I'm your room-mate *and* a mermaid."

"Yeah, not your best lie. You're also admin on all our social."

"Shit. I need chocolate and caffeine." She veered right, up to the campus cafe's walk-thru window and ordered a mochaccino.

"It's odd she didn't know that in advance," Zig said. "It would've been easy to check."

"Sloppy work on her part, but listen," Misty lowered her voice to a whisper while the equipment inside whirred, "she suspects Paul Quaid, has from the beginning."

"The husband," Zig said, and Misty nodded hard. "But they ruled him out."

"She knows that, she was the cop on the case. But Zig, she must know something we don't. She thinks there's evidence in the cabin, but she can't get a search warrant."

The barista set her order on the counter. Misty ran her card, took her cup, and tasted her first sip.

"Plain coffee," Zig said. "Black and bitter, just like me."

Misty choke-laughed and spat chocolatey goodness into empty space. No casualties.

Zig rolled her eyes. She took her cup and ran her card, and they walked toward the emptiest spot with a bench, way off to the left under the willows. Misty sat down on the bench when they reached it, but Zig stood, pacing every now and then.

"That's not all, Zig. Mackey has a photo of him and Eva,

and he's looking at her like he wants to, I don't know, *own* her."

Zig stopped pacing. "As in screw her?"

She nodded, tapping her phone to bring up the photo, then handed it to Zig. "See?"

"Ew." She frowned and spread the photo bigger. "Was Earl Mackey secretly in lust with his mermaid?" she asked in her dulcet podcaster voice. "Was her marriage to another man more than he could take?"

"We need to find out whether that cop investigated Mackey at all. They seemed to be friends. But what was *his* alibi for the time when Eva disappeared?"

"Agree, agree." Zig nodded hard and started pacing again. "But all that should be in the police reports, right? And that's in progress."

"Yeah."

"So, then we keep digging into the husband."

"I can't believe I'm saying this, Zig, but we have to get a look inside that cabin. Detective Scott was adamant that if she could get in there, she could find proof."

"It would be illegal," Zig said.

"I know."

"You're dating a cop, though."

"I know. I've been thinking about that."

"And it would have to be this weekend, you know that too, right?"

"*This* weekend?" Misty asked.

"So, you're okay with the breaking and entering, just not with the timing?"

"I—" Misty was dying to get inside the Quaid cabin. "Yeah. That's exactly what I'm saying. Does it have to be this weekend?"

"It's the weekend of the art show," Zig said. "He goes every year." She paced back and forth with her coffee in one hand, taking sips as if to fuel her thoughts. "It can't be coincidence, can it? Them taking another look at the husband after all this time, on the tenth anniversary of her disappearance?"

"And just when we've launched the podcast," Misty said. "It's stirring all this up again, the cop said."

"Our podcast is?" Zig stopped pacing and met Misty's eyes.

Misty looked right back at her and grinned. "They were talking about it on campus radio this morning."

"Whaaaa...?" She smiled so hard Misty could see all her braces. "This is good. This is so good for us!"

"Good for us, as long as we don't piss the cops off too much," Misty said. "We should probably try to make nice with the detective if we can. Maybe offer to share evidence."

"Or at least pretend to share evidence," Zig agreed, nodding fast. "But right now, our priority is to get a look inside Paul Quaid's cabin. And listen, if we're doing this, we can't get caught."

"Damn right we can't. My boyfriend's a cop."

Zig lowered her head and ran a hand over her braids, then looked up again. "You have to keep him from getting tangled up in our shit. You know that, right?" Zig said. "He's a rookie. You could screw his career."

"I know."

"Are you sure you want to do this?"

"I'm sure." And she was. She was surprised by just how sure she was. But she was also thinking about Jeremy. Zig was right. If she was going to push the boundaries of legality, she really had to keep him far away from it. At least until it was over. "So, what's the plan?"

"We leave our cell phones behind, so there's no sign we ever left Saratoga Springs. We'll leave the car somewhere and hike in. That cabin is right at the edge of a state forest. We should bring camping gear in case we have to stay overnight." She finally sat down. "We'll stake the place out all weekend if we have to. We'll stay until he leaves. Then we go inside and see if there's evidence."

Misty said, "We don't take anything. We just photograph it."

"Photograph, yes," Zig said. "We won't have phones, so we'll pick up one of those throw-away cameras."

Misty thought the whole thing through and nodded slowly. "It's a good plan," she said. "It's also the worst possible weekend. There are shows, and it's not like I can just get someone to fill in."

"Isn't it, though?" Zig lowered her glasses and looked at Misty over the tops of their red frames. "Isn't it actually *just* like that?"

"You really think what I do is that easy?"

"No, I do not think it's easy. What I *do* think is that an identical twin could fake her way through it for one freaking weekend."

Misty pressed her lips. She and Zig had been working on this thing for weeks. They'd pored over every article written on the case in preparation for this. They'd filed a FOIA request for the police report. This case and their podcast meant a lot to her. But so did her job.

But it was that, a job. Being a mermaid in a fancy dinner club was not going to be her career.

"It's okay if you can't," Zig said. "I know this isn't as serious to you as it is to me, so—"

"It's serious enough to me that I added two electives to my already-packed summer session. Crime Scene Processing and Observational Skills for Investigators."

Zig smiled wide, then bit it back, then gave up trying. "You did?"

"Revised schedule is on my desk. You can see for yourself when we head back." Then she sighed, and her heart felt heavy as hell.

"I know it's gotta be hard to ask your sister," Zig said. "Especially when you can't tell her why."

"I can't tell her why?"

Zig made her eyes wider and shook her head firmly left, then right. "Not cop-guy either. Nobody gets to know anything that hasn't aired yet. Ever. That's a deal breaker. Agree?"

Misty bit her lip, then nodded once, firmly. "I can do that. I can ask Christy to fill in for my shows this weekend, and I can keep my reasons to myself." She closed her eyes. "It's gonna be harder to deal with Jeremy. But I can't risk his career for my... budding new passion."

"Passion huh?"

"Yeah. I really love working on this thing with you, Zig. I like reading the reports and picking out clues and testing out theories. I love writing the scripts for the show."

"Your scripts are fantastic," Zig said. "You're good at it. A natural. And your writing is way better than mine."

"Runs in the family," Misty said.

RACHEL

"She did *what*?" I could not believe what my adult son from another mother was saying by way of my cell phone.

Christy's eventual reply to my urgent text had been:

Christy: Misty is fine and also an adult."

Sounded snarky AF to me.

So today I'd called Jere to pick his brain about Misty again, in hopes of easing her mother's mind, and got the shock of my life. "She broke up with you?" I asked more softly.

"Taking a break, is how she put it," Jeremy said. His voice was an octave lower than usual. Poor kid. "They tell you at the academy that relationships with cops are hard, but I never thought—"

"That isn't it," I said.

"What do you mean? What do you... do you know something? Are you like... *getting* something?"

"No, I'm not *getting* something."

Other than a pair of drowned nieces and a dead mermaid.

Shut up, Inner Bitch.

"Maybe she met somebody." His voice sounded dead. "It's fine. She's young."

"You're the same age."

"I'm a lot."

"*She's* a lot." I wanted to wrap him up and hug him and smack my niece upside the head. "Something's up with her, Jeremy. I don't think this is about you."

"When someone dumps you, it's about you, Aunt Rache."

I was worried and I didn't believe in beating around the bush. "Don't make this a reason to drink. If anything, it's a reason not to."

"I'm not drinking." I knew there was more, so I stayed quiet and waited for it. Phone calls were so much easier than in-person discussions. I was way more not-fucking-psychic without visual input flooding my brain. "I'm thinking about drinking," he said at length. And then, after another long pause, "I went to a meeting after work last night. I'm going again tonight."

"Do you want to come home? Stay in your old room for a couple of weeks? You could commute to work with your uncle. Myrtle would be over the moon."

"I might take you up on that. But you're going out to Saratoga Springs, right?"

"Yeah, I had Mason book us a room for the weekend. I was going to ask Amy to stay with Myrtle and work out of my office, but she had a lot going on." It was a lie. My over-worked and overpaid right hand woman would've been happy as hell to bulldog-sit at my place for the weekend. I felt Jeremy doubting how real my need was. I'd also felt the little spark of life in his heart when I'd said the word "home."

"You'd be doing me a huge favor, you know," I went on. "Myrtle would be so much more comfortable with you here. Amy overnight is not normal, and you know how easily upset she is. She'll have a tough enough time with us being gone."

I had him. I knew it even before the sigh left his lungs. "Okay. When are you leaving?"

"Given the latest development, I want to head out there early tomorrow morning."

"Because she dumped me," he said.

"She called it a break, not a break*up*. And, by the way, I haven't told either of the girls our weekend plans. Christy would rat us out to Misty if she knew. Sandra's keeping it to herself too, or at least, that's the plan."

"Your sister is not the best at keeping secrets, unlike..." He trailed off and my antennae quivered.

"Unlike her daughter. Unlike Misty. Was that what you almost said?"

"Um... yeah. But this has to stay between the two of us, Rache, cause I don't know what it means. But... she's apparently working at someplace called The Sapphire Club. She left a paystub in my car last time we hung out."

"I thought she was working at the campus café," I said.

"So did I," Jeremy said.

"So does her mother," I added.

"You can't tell her," he said quickly. "It has to stay

between us. I haven't even gone online to check the place out. It feels over the line, now that we're—"

"On a break," I said before he could finish.

"Yeah. Whatever."

My heart ached for him. "Anyway," I said, "it gives me something to go on. I'll keep it to myself, but you know it's going to come out. You can't keep secrets in this family."

He nodded. "It's probably not what it sounds like."

"That's good, because it sounds like the kind of place with poles. But it can't be that. Everybody knows Misty's the good twin."

"Maybe she's sick of being the good twin."

I sighed. "I don't think that's it. Seriously, Jere, don't jump to conclusions. Be a cop. Wait for evidence. And I'll go find some answers before we both go off the deep end. We'll only be gone two or three nights. If you have to go to work, I'll have Amy on standby for backup bulldog-sitting. You have her number." I sighed, and added, "But I hope you stick around after we get back. You know, if you want to."

"I think I will. Home is a good place to lick my wounds."

"Myrtle will help you out with that," I said, glancing at my dog, who was lying across my feet on the sofa, snoring loudly enough that Jeremy could hear her, too.

"I'll see you when we get back."

"Okay."

I didn't hang up, because he had more to say, and then he did. "Thanks for being there, Aunt Rache. All this time. I mean it."

"I got the best end of that deal, kid. Go be a good cop."

He was done. I hung up and twisted my nose in a

sidewinder sniffle. Twenty-two, rookie cop, and he could still make me bawl. The little shit.

I still had to pack. I leaned over and squished Myrt's face between my hands and kissed her nose.

She was going to be majorly pissed at us when we got back.

RACHEL

Mason drove our bright red Solterra, which had replaced my beloved Crosstrek. He still had his Beast, and I still had my T-Bird, but we only broke the gas-burners out on special occasions these days. He knew a lot was up with me, but he also knew I'd tell him when I was ready.

"So, it's not really a dress-shopping trip?" he asked, glancing sideways at me.

"Oh, no, it totally is. I know *exactly* which dress I want to try on."

The tension left Mason's face like the sun coming out on a cloudy day. Aw, man. Was he worried about us? I wasn't doing a very good job as a partner if I he was. "But since I'm going to be out there finding a dress good enough to marry you in, it's also an excuse to check up on Misty."

"Because she dumped Jeremy," he reiterated.

"It's a break. And yes. And also because she's stopped coming home from school on weekends and is keeping secrets, such as the fact that she's working at someplace called The Sapphire Club. Where we have dinner reservations."

"Under a false name?" he was teasing. His dimples showed.

"I felt like that would be overkill. But I reserved under Brown. No first names. Maybe she won't notice."

"Sneaky."

"It sounds like a strip club, doesn't it?"

He shot me a surprised look, then gave his head a shake. "Come on. Misty? No way."

"I know, I know. But why keep it a secret?"

He took a long nasal breath, and his eyes fell closed very briefly. "So, we're spying on a grown woman because her mom and aunt are worried."

"Her mom has a bad feeling. And who the hell am I to question mother's intuition? There's more shit in the world than just *my* shit."

"That's profound, Rache. You have such a way with words."

I stuck out my tongue at him, and he laughed. But then I went serious again. "The twins have something like my stuff. Just between them."

"I know. I've seen it."

"You have?"

"Yeah. I swear to God, one day at Sandra's, Misty got up and went to the front door as Christy was just pulling up out front. And remember that time Josh was throwing rocks into the reservoir and hit Christy right in the head? Misty yelped as if she felt it."

"Yes! But she didn't even see it happen, she was looking the other way."

He nodded. "I thought I was imagining things. Glad you've noticed it, too."

"Yeah, I have." I sighed. "I asked Christy what's up with Misty, for what good that did."

"She would never tell you," Mason said. "Not if it's something Misty doesn't want us to know."

"True."

We drove in comfortable silence for a while. I glanced over at him, and he looked back and his eyes did that thing they did sometimes. They went all soft and dreamy. Nobody in my life had ever looked at me the way Mason did. Everything he felt for me was in that look.

"I can't wait to be your wife," I said. "You know that, right?"

"There's no hurry. No pressure, Rache."

"I know." I nodded, took a breath. "My stuff's been acting weird, and I don't know what's wrong. I'm a little freaked out, to be honest."

"Acting weird how?"

"Mermaids," I said. "I keep seeing mermaids. One mermaid, really. I think she might be dead."

"That's... weird."

"It sure the fuck is. But it's worse than that."

"The wedding nightmare," he said, nodding slowly. "You said you couldn't remember it, but you know I can tell when you're lying."

"It was... too awful to tell you, Mace. But it's too awful not to tell you, too."

He nodded.

I squeezed my eyes closed and the full nightmare returned, washing over me like a tsunami. I saw it as clearly as if I were there, just as I had the first time I'd dreamed it. The sun was glinting off the blue water of the reservoir. Mason and I stood in front of a wooden arch all wrapped in grapevines and tiny purple and white flowers. I didn't know what the flowers were. They looked like the violets that grew wild on the back lawn.

Part of my thought was that I should look to see what we were wearing, but I was quickly distracted by the lawn full of guests. They sat in rows of wooden folding chairs with red cushioned seats. My sister Sandra was right in front, beside our parents, who'd died long ago. And on the groom's side, there was Mason's mother, Elizabeth, and his brother. His dead serial-killer brother whose donated corneas had restored my eyesight seven years ago. What was he doing at our wedding?

Jeremy and Joshua were standing in the back of the crowd, and our house was behind them. They were standing oddly, though, hands clasped in front of them, legs wide for stability, stoic expressions on their faces. Like they weren't really in there. Like these were tin soldiers without souls, guarding the event.

I looked at Mason again and fell into his eyes and loved him from my toes. And then my sister made a sound like a stepped-on puppy. A yelp. A cry, and I shot my eyes to hers, but she wasn't looking at me. She was looking past me, toward the reservoir, and then she rose, and pointed, and screamed in a way that made my ears bleed as I turned my head in slow motion.

I didn't want to turn. I had to force my head to turn. It felt as if the pivots in my neck had locked up. I pushed and pushed, and my neck hurt, but I turned to see what was making my sister cry.

The other guests were on their feet, shouting and surging in slow motion toward the reservoir. I was aware of them, even though I wasn't facing them. I was finally facing the water. There, beside our familiar dock, in the gravel-bottomed shallows, lay two girls, facedown. Misty's long blond hair swam and moved with the motion of the water, floating this way and that with each little wave that came in. Christy's was shorter and dark, plastered to her head but not hiding her face like Misty's did. I could see her pale skin, her parted lips, her open, lifeless eyes.

It was too much. I opened my eyes and looked at Mason. He had pulled over onto the shoulder of the road and was staring at me in shock. "*Our* girls?" he asked, so I guessed I'd narrated the dream aloud.

I nodded.

"Misty and Christy?"

"Yeah."

"Holy..." He pushed one hand from his forehead back, ruffling his hair. "No wonder you've been dragging your feet on wedding plans."

"Yeah. But... it wasn't like my usual stuff. It wasn't *anything* like my usual stuff. It was more like a normal nightmare. I guess. I think."

"Well, that's good. Could it be like... nerves?"

"Why would I be nervous?" I reached across to slide my hand over his on the steering wheel. "We're already married, Mason. All we're doing with this wedding is celebrating it and making it legal."

He met my eyes, nodded slow. "That's how I look at it, too. That's why if you don't want to do that part—"

"I *do* want to do that part," I told him. "We just might have to do it while holding our girls between us to make sure they stay safe."

"Yeah," he said with a nervous laugh. Then, "But it wasn't like your usual stuff, though. Maybe it was just a normal, garden-variety nightmare."

"Maybe. Except Sandra's nervous too."

"Not to be discounted."

"The mermaid was just like my normal stuff, though. I did a ride-along in her head, trapped in a fish tank. Banged my head so hard I still have a phantom ache." I rubbed the spot when I said it.

"But... mermaids aren't real."

He said it like he was testing to make sure I still knew that. "No, mermaids are not real," I said. "And yet, my worried sister brought me this today. Unprompted." I pulled the chain on my neck, lifting the steel mermaid from my jacket to show him.

He looked at it, then looked again. "Is that a—?"

"Mermaid. With a rape whistle and shit. She got the girls each one, too. I mean, come on, this is bizarre, right? That she'd choose a mermaid after I had that dream? It's not just me."

"It's not just you."

I sighed in relief. "I'm glad you came with me. You're my other half, Mace. You always have my back."

"Always will, too," he said. "No matter what." He pulled me in for a long, strong, powerful hug that filled me with everything I needed in that moment. Everything I need in any moment.

Then he pulled the car into motion, and we continued our journey.

CHAPTER 5

RACHEL

After handing our keys over to a valet, we walked through a dark-stained split rail fence into a garden paradise to the stained-glass sidelights bracketing double entry doors. I bet they would light right up when it wasn't pitch dark behind them.

Right then it was so dim I couldn't even make out their design. A stylized wooden sign with "Wedding Grounds" burned into its wood, pointed toward the back. I had to peer around the building to see more gardens, greenery and paths spilling from just beyond the back parking lot all the way to the lakeshore.

"It doesn't look like a strip club," I said with hope in my voice.

Then the clouds moved, and the world brightened. Shafts of sunlight spilled down onto us, chased each other up the flagstone path and illuminated the glorious stained-glass sidelights.

Facing each other in a blissful pose, heads lowered, eyes closed, holding lilies to their noses with their hair flowing behind them, were two beautiful stained-glass mermaids, one blonde, one brunette.

My heart tripped over itself in my chest. Mason put his arm around my shoulders and squeezed. "Steady."

We walked through the stained-glass mermaid doors into large a darkened room. The walls were ebony wood with patches of stonework. The room was filled with dining tables. There were diners at many of them. The right wall held a long bar, and the very front of the room held a blue velvet curtain.

"Is that a *stage*? Is that a fucking *stage*?"

"It's *Misty*," Mason reminded me. "Come on."

A beautiful young woman in a dress with blue and silver sequins that shimmered when she moved, greeted us with a smile and an armful of menus.

Yes! Inner Bitch cried. *Food!*

"Welcome to The Sapphire Club. Follow me."

She led the way, shimmering. I caught up and tapped her shoulder. "Something in the back." I pointed to a shadowy cove to the left. "Like that over there."

"Oh, sure thing." She shimmered in that direction and soon we were sliding into a half-circle booth with a full view of the stage. As she handed us the menus and said our server would be right over, I noticed there wasn't a seat in the place without a full view of the stage. And then I noticed the crowd.

This was definitely not a strip-club sort of a crowd. What the hell was Misty *doing*? Stand-up?

Our waiter arrived. He was a freckle-faced redhead who wasn't wearing a shirt, and he was jacked.

And suddenly it looks like a strip club again.

Shut up, Inner Bitch.

"I'm Malcolm and I'll be taking care of you this evening. Can I start you off with an appetizer?"

"Is this a strip club?" I blurted.

"*Whaaat?*" His eyes were green. I noticed because they widened so much. "No!"

"Just checking. I'll have the buffet," I said, and handed it to the shocked and semi-nude waiter.

"Um... there's no buffet." He put the menu down in front of me. "I'll come back."

"No, don't do that. I'm starved and I need a drink. Vodka Diet." I'd tossed every trace of alcohol from our place in honor or Jeremy's visit. We'd been a dry house for as long as he'd lived at home, but now that he was on his own, I kept a little stash around. "And appetizers..." I opened the menu, looked at it and pointed at a gigantic sampler platter. "That's a start."

"Beer," Mason said. "Whatever's on tap. And the pasta primavera looks good."

"Make it two," I said.

"Drinks and appetizer will be right out. We don't serve during the show, which is going to start in ten minutes, so you get the rest right after. That okay?"

"Sure," Mason said. I was going to blurt that I would die of starvation by then. He really was so much nicer than I.

A taller waiter with a shirt on brought our drinks almost instantly, the appetizers minutes later. We took our time with them as I checked every table, every server, the bartender, the bussers, but there was no sign of Misty. If she worked there, she either worked in the kitchen or on that stage.

Halfway through the appetizers, the lights flashed on, then off, then on, then off entirely. The room was completely dark, and the curtains rose in slow-mo. The crowd went quiet, and you could feel the anticipation that slow-rising drape was causing. Ethereal music came up. I glimpsed something behind the curtain. Blue. Wavy. Water?

A fish tank, Inner Bitch said. *Like the one the mermaid was in.*

A huge tank of water stretched across the front of the room.

The lights within came on, and there was a collective gasp as an underwater paradise was illuminated before our eyes. Giant sea plants, some with huge blooms, swayed in the currents, boulders and corals created a landscape with hills and valleys in miniature.

Kinda like the one where your dream mermaid was trapped, isn't it?

Not exactly like it, though, I thought. But I wasn't sure. I tried to recall it to mind, but honestly, I wasn't sure. There'd been a shipwreck behind her, hadn't there? Movement caught my attention— a mermaid came swimming into view. She had dozens of long sable braids that flowed behind her, and an elaborate white tail and bikini top against her dark skin. There were frilly, scaly fins on her forearms, and sparkles on her cheeks. The crowd applauded as she performed a series of graceful flips and turns, and eventually swam right up to the glass, eyes wide open, smiling brightly, and waved.

Cheers erupted, and she swam away out of sight.

Mason closed his hand around my fist on the seat between us when another mermaid came swimming into sight, way in the back of the tank where you could hardly see her. This one had long blond hair. I made out purple and teal in her tail, and her top was two iridescent purple oyster shells. Eventually, she looked up as if someone above was talking to her, then she swam forward a little, shrugged, and performed a somersault by spinning her arms out at her sides like a fourth grader in a swimming pool. On the final flip, she hit herself in the head with her tail, and rolled her expressive eyes as she stumbled into the light. She smiled with bubbles coming out between her teeth and peered out at the crowd through squinty eyes.

"Misty?" Mason whispered. And then he said, "No. That's not Misty."

"It's Christy," I said. And then I added, "What the actual fuck?"

Rachel: I'm at table six. Get your tail out here.

That was my text to Christy's phone two seconds after the curtain lowered on the pretty, oversized fish tank. My hands were shaking so hard it took me three tries to send it. I'd gone ice cold.

"I've got you," Mason said.

"I know."

It's not the same aquarium, Inner Bitch whispered inside my mind. *It's not the same as the one in the ride-along.*

It wasn't the same, not exactly. I called the memory of that vision up. The bottom had been lined in blue gravel. This one had what looked like sand lining the bottom, with sunken treasures sticking up out of it: a golden goblet, a pocket watch, jewelry, along with natural treasures like seashells and corals and sparkling silver stones. The tank in my memory had a ruined castle, leafless tendrils of waving seaweed, and two boulders; the tank in front of my eyes had leafy, flowering plants dancing around it. And two boulders.

Are those rocks the same? I think they might be the same.

I don't know, Inner Bitch. A rock is a rock.

But I knew very well they could've changed the layout a dozen times in ten years. I pulled my attention from the watery depths to watch my phone, but no reply came. Our food did. I sampled the offerings on my plate, moving on autopilot while my stomach warned me not to even think about sending any of it down. I tasted every item anyway. Then my phone finally chirped.

> Christy: What are you doing here?

> Rachel: You didn't return my call.

Christy: So you show just show up?

Rachel: Yes, I just show up. What are you doing here? And where is your sister?

I tapped my finger on the table and waited.

Christy: ...

Shirtless came back. "Can you bring another place setting? Our mermaid's joining us."

Christy: ...

Rachel: Christy, answer me right now.

My thumbs tapped the screen so hard they made noise. But only the ellipses appeared in reply as our confused waiter hurried away. He came back with a plate and a set of utensils, but wisely retreated without a word while I drummed my fingers on the table and stared at the phone, impatience radiating from my very being.

The phone pinged at last.

Christy: I'm coming already! It takes time to get out of that tail.

"I bet it does," I said aloud. Then I turned my phone face down on the table, sighed heavily and took a long sip of my alcoholic beverage. Nothing was wrong. No one was in danger. No one had died.

As I lowered my glass, the mermaid from my vision

surfaced, glared at me from brown eyes within a jungle of brunette curls, and vanished again.

Okay, so maybe someone *had* died.

"Rache?" Mason covered my hand— the one that was holding the glass a few inches from my nose while I blinked at its remaining contents. There were only ice cubes and a swizzle stick with a seashell on top.

I set the glass down, took a deep breath. "Good. I'm good."

"I wonder why Christy is performing as a mermaid?" Mason asked.

I focused on our food as a distraction from the knot of worry in my stomach and used a celery stalk to scoop up some spinach and avocado dip. Maybe eating would settle the queasiness in my stomach. "Taking Misty's place," I said.

"How do you know that?"

"Did her *see* her in there? Compared to the others? It was obviously her first time."

"Gee, thanks, Aunt Rache."

I looked up with a dip-dripping celery stalk halfway to my lips. There was my Christy, still wearing the ridiculous blonde wig, wet and twisted into a knot at the back of her head. She was a short-and-sassy brunette these days. She'd washed off the dramatic mermaid makeup and reapplied her usual dark shadow and not much else. Her elfin face had lost its teenage plumpness. The exquisite bone structure showed through now. She was a grown-ass woman. When the hell had it happened?

Shirtless returned with a chair, placing it at the open end, with its back toward the once-again closed stage curtains. I noticed the way his skin shimmered in the light this time. Now that I wasn't looking for signs of a strip-joint, it was obvious the wait staff were merfolk, too. Demi-merfolk, maybe. After all, you couldn't wait tables with a tail.

"Hey, Misty," Shirtless said. Then more softly, "You okay?"

"Why wouldn't I be okay?" she asked. Then she bit her lip, made her voice a half octave higher and *way* kinder, and added, "Of course I'm okay. I mean... I pulled a muscle prac-ticing, I think."

"Ohhh, that explains it." But he was looking at her face and frowning a little harder.

"Malcolm, how 'bout that refill?" I tapped my empty glass. It had the desired effect. He stopped looking at my niece and looked at me instead.

"Sorry, Ma'am. I uh— I'll be right back."

"See you later, Malcolm," Christy said in the most Misty way she could. She'd added a cheerful lilt that would've fooled her own mother on the phone. Wouldn't have fooled me.

Christy reached for the appetizer tray, and I put my hand over of hers. "First, talk. Where is your sister?"

"I don't know." She pulled her hand away, then used the serving fork to stab several appetizers at once and shook them onto her plate. "She's a grown woman. If she wants to take off for a weekend, why do you care?"

"I'm here. You know me well enough to know that I have a reason to be here. *Talk.*"

Christy sent a look to Mason as if in search of support. He

said, "Don't you think, Christy, that if Rachel is worried, you should be worried too?"

That seemed to get her off her high horse. She frowned, making little creases between her brows.

"Where is your sister?" I said, gesturing with my unbitten celery stalk. "Why is she working here and keeping it secret? Why are you taking her place and not telling anyone? What the ever-loving fuck is going on?"

Christy closed her eyes, took a breath, and pressed her palms to the table on either side of her plate. "Okay, okay. Misty asked me to cover for her for the weekend and not to tell anyone. And let me tell you something, I am a *saint* to do it, because it's *way* harder than it looks, and I can't hold my breath that long."

"Yeah, you're sister of the year," I said, then emphasizing each word, "Where is she?"

"I told you, I don't know." She lowered her eyes. I swear to God, I wanted to shake her. "Look, I mean it," she rushed on. "I don't know where she is. She said not to ask questions, that she'd tell me when she was ready, but that it was important to her. One of the most important things ever, she said. But... I got the feeling," her gaze slid Mason's way, "she's with a guy."

"A guy?" Mason asked. "As in, a not-Jeremy guy?"

"Jeremy says they're on a break," I reminded him. And Christy didn't seem surprised. She'd known, then. "He said that was her decision, not his, so as unlikely as it seems, another guy would track." I nodded at Christy. "What else did she say?"

"Nothing, she wouldn't say where she was going, just that she'd be back Monday morning."

"What else did she say?" I asked again, saying the words slower this time so she would know I wanted it word for word.

She closed her eyes in that slow way that meant, "You are really pissing me off" without a word. I knew that look. Hell, I *invented* that look. "She said she had to pack, that they were leaving soon."

"They," I repeated.

"Yeah. And she said she wouldn't have cell service."

"Word for word, Christy. Did she say she was going somewhere without cell service?"

She moved her eyes left and right, not looking at anything, but looking for a memory. "She said 'I won't be reachable by cell phone until I get back. So don't worry if you can't get me.' And she said not to breathe a word to anyone. She gave me one private mermaiding lesson in the middle of the night—"

Mason cut her off with, "How the hell did you get in here in the middle of the—"

"The performers all have keys," she interrupted right back. "They have to rehearse after hours, so—"

"Not reachable by cell," I repeated, shutting them both up.

Mason met my eyes and nodded. "We can work with that."

"No," Christy said, "you can't." She swung her gaze between us. "Misty and I are adult women. We live on our own. We get to have private lives and you don't get to go snooping in them just because we want a couple of days alone. Jesus, you guys, let go already." She sat back in her chair. "Do you mind if I eat now?"

I decided to try to enjoy my meal instead of glaring at her, because if I didn't, she was going to eat it all. In between bites, I said, "Do you think she and Jeremy are over?"

"How would I know? It's none of my business." Christy kept eating.

"You're being a bitch, you know that?"

"You were being a bitch first." She ate three more appetizers, then shoved her chair back and rose. "Nice visit. I'm outta here. I've done my duty for the family tonight. Have a nice drive back."

"Christy." She turned to walk away, so I had no choice. "I dreamt about a mermaid before I knew about this place. Don't tell your mother."

She turned and met my eyes. I nodded once. She knew the kind of dreams I meant. But just to drive it home, I said, "We are not here on a fucking lark, and we're not here to pry.

She lowered her head for a second, then she sat back down. "Do you think Misty's in... danger?"

"I don't know. That's what we came to find out."

She seemed to search inwardly. "She seemed fine. Better than fine, really. She seemed excited. I think she's okay." She reached for a popper, took a bite and chewed as if the jaw motion powered the gears in her brain. "You guys want to see behind the scenes after we eat? It's actually pretty cool, if you're not the one wearing the tail." She reached for another appetizer and dropped her mini backpack on the arm of the chair again, but she missed. It hit the floor, toppled side-ways, and things fell out near my feet.

I bent to help gather them and came up with the large metal mermaid on the end of a silver chain— the Crisis Companion. I straightened, holding it up.

"Mom's insane," she said. "She got us both these crazy things."

"She got you mermaids," I said. "Knowing nothing about this place," I waved an open hand, "she got you mermaids."

Christy's eyebrows bent. "That *is* weird, now that you mention it."

"Weirder yet that it's in the bottom of your bag with hairy scrunchies, loose change, and makeup crumbs." I put the chain over her head. "Fucking wear it. It goes with the getup anyway."

"It'll float up and hit me in the teeth."

"That thing won't *float* anywhere. Trust me. I got one too." I pulled my mermaid out from under my blouse on her chain. "And I wear it, because I love my sister, and when she sees me wearing it, she is reminded of that."

She closed her big, expressive blue eyes slowly. "I hear you. I'll wear it."

"It's hard on parents when their kids grow up," I said.

"Harder on the kids," she muttered. But she put the neck-lace on. I didn't really think we needed to wear them, except from time to time in Sandra's presence. But mine was growing on me, and making the brat wear hers was a lovely little bit of revenge.

You're welcome, Sis, I thought.

MISTY

"I can't believe I let you talk me into this." Misty slid another long, bendy, sectioned rod through a set of the dome tent's sewn-in pockets. They had both done so until they had what looked like a flattened spider on the ground in front of them. The rods, or whatever, stuck out way past the tent fabric. "There's no way this is gonna work."

"Tell me you've never pitched a tent without telling me you've never pitched a tent," Zig said. Then, with a nod, "Grab that end."

Misty took the end of the pole. Zig took its opposite end across the fabric from her. "Now, tuck it into that little pocket in the tent fabric. You see it?"

She looked down, she saw it, and slid end of the rod into the pocket, but she had to slide it way in to do so, so it was sticking out even further on Zig's side. "Now what?"

"They bend for a reason, Misty. Didn't your parents ever take you camping?"

"Sure, but they never made me pitch the tent."

"Well they should've." She gripped the pole thingy and pulled its end toward the pocket, making the entire thing bow outward and sliding the fabric pockets lower, as she snapped the end into its pocket. "Next pole," she said.

In two minutes, they had a dome-shaped tent set up. Its green and brown camouflage pattern was not reassuring. They didn't look anything like the pines around them. She unzipped the tent, took her backpack inside, and opened it up.

It smelled good in the woods. They'd parked a ways off, hiked about a mile through state forest to get to the cabin where Eva Quaid had lived with her husband, Paul.

Zig had scoped out the spot ahead of time, a small clearing, tucked in among dense pines, on a steep ridge with an excellent view of the cabin. A little brook tumbled along beside it. The place was pretty rustic, nice. Its red-brown logs matched the tree trunks in the woods all around it. The roof was green, and so were the shutters, and so were the surrounding pines. Its "lawn" was scattered plants in a substrate entirely made of pine needles. It smelled like Christmas on steroids out there.

"This place is amazing," she said, taking a big deep breath of it. "No wonder the guy hardly ever leaves it. Who'd want to?"

Zig was unrolling her sleeping bag inside the tent. "Are you kidding me right now? Middle of nowhere, off the grid? There's a pic of this place in the dictionary definition of 'serial killer's lair.'"

"Not off the grid." Misty pointed at power lines, and then the satellite dish on the roof.

"Middle of nowhere still applies." Zig placed her sleeping bag to the left of center in the circular space inside the tent, pulled a mini pillow out of her bag and tucked it into place.

"Don't get so comfortable," Misty said. She didn't unroll her own bag. "We won't have to spend the night. He'll leave soon."

"I don't know," Zig said. "When I go on a road trip, I leave in the morning. He hasn't budged all day."

With their gear inside, they returned to the log right at the edge of their site. Beyond the log, the ground dropped down sharply, its face gnarly roots and red earth. At the bottom, twenty feet down, the stream burbled happily past. Misty imagined it absorbing any noise they made up here. Past the stream, in the middle of a clearing, was the Quaid cabin.

It was like a storybook painting. Or one of those by that Kincaid guy her mom liked. She handed Zig the binoculars and got up to stretch her legs.

They'd been watching the place for hours. As the day waned and Paul Quaid still showed no sign of leaving, they'd finally decided to pitch their tent.

Misty was itching to get a closer look, but the man was still there. He'd wandered in and out a few times, moving between the house and the little slab-sided outbuilding she presumed was his workshop. He'd spent hours in there, pounding on things and welding. At several points the workshop's windows had blazed with white-light, and his hammering rang through the woods for what must have been miles.

Eventually he returned to the house again, and the smells of food cooking wafted up to tease their senses as the sun vanished behind the trees.

Dark came earlier in the woods. Misty was glad they'd pitched the tent while it was still light enough to see what they were doing.

"He worked on his art all day," she said. "He *must* be going to the show. He hasn't missed one in fifteen years, according to our research. Maybe he just wasn't ready yet. But he's definitely going."

"Yeah. In the morning." Even as Zig said the words, they came true; the lights in the cabin went out, first in that little room in the front, and then in the back. Zig sighed and lowered the spyglasses.

Misty said, "You're right. He's gone to bed."

"It's not even nine yet." Zig rolled her eyes. "Old people."

"Christy will have already performed," Misty said softly. She pictured her badass sister playing a mermaid and couldn't quite make the vision appear. She hoped someone got video. "I can't even text and ask how it went."

"If we had our phones, and anything went wrong, they could prove we were here. You know this." Zig sighed. "He'll leave in the morning. I'm betting on it. But I think it's safe to assume he's not going anywhere tonight."

"He was working in that room with the little windows for a long time this morning," Misty said. Zig would know which room she meant. Front, far left. "And he was messing around in there again when he went in at lunch time."

"I wonder if that's the room Detective Scott wants to get a look at," Zig said.

"I'd lay money on it." Misty gnawed her lip. "What if he doesn't go this year?"

"He'll go."

"But maybe this year is different. Detective Scott said we'd stirred things up with the podcast. And it's the tenth anniversary."

"What I wouldn't give for a copy of that police report," Zig said.

"We filed a FOIA. We'll get it."

"We could get it sooner." Zig wiggled her eyebrows. "Your boyfriend's a cop."

Misty lowered her eyes fast. "We're on a break."

"What, now?" Zig came off the log, binoculars hanging from her neck. She turned around, trying to catch Misty's eyes, but Misty avoided them. "Why?"

Misty shook her head and didn't answer.

"Is it because of the podcast?" Zig asked.

She finally met her friend's eyes. "He's a cop. He's always wanted to be a cop, and now he is one, but he's a rookie. They're not gonna look the other way if he starts getting involved in our... Jeeze, Zig, we're gonna break and enter as soon as Paul Quaid leaves his house."

"But you're nuts about the guy!" Zig pushed a hand over her braids and turned in a slow circle. "Maybe you shouldn't stay. Maybe I never should've got you involved in all this. Maybe—"

"I want to stay," Misty said. "The breakup it's— just for now. Just so I can see..." She stopped, shook her head, started over. "Let me handle my relationship issues myself, okay, Zig? Let's focus on what we're here to do."

Zig blinked, clearly surprised. Misty was not normally assertive. "Okay."

"Good." Misty nodded. "Now, to business. If Quaid doesn't leave in the morning—"

"He will," Zig cut in.

"If he doesn't, we won't get a better chance to see what's in that room than right now," Misty said, "and I want to see what the hell is in there."

"*Dayum*." Zig was looking at her like they'd never met. "You're seriously into this, aren't you?"

She hesitated, then nodded. "More than I expected to be. Enough so that I'm... rethinking who I am. What I want. I'm excited. I can't remember when I've been this excited about anything."

"Did *I* do all that?"

She shrugged one shoulder. "I don't think it was entirely you," she said, but she didn't elaborate. She'd never considered herself a crime-solver. That was what her aunt Rachel did, and Uncle Mason, and Jeremy now, too. But somehow, the moment Zig had asked for her help, some previously dormant gene had awakened in her, and it refused to go back to sleep. "I think we should sneak down there and look through those little windows, just in case it's our only chance."

"It's pitch dark in there," Zig said. "It's not like we can aim a flashlight beam through the windows, and it's... oh, wow. That's handy."

She had turned in a circle of frustration and stopped, facing their tent, behind them. Misty turned to see what she was talking about. The upper curve of a bright white moon was shining in between the pines. When it rose above the trees, it would beam right down on the cabin.

Misty grinned at Zig. "That moonlight will be flooding right through those windows in a little while. Like a spotlight. Like it's meant to be." And then she started to follow the tree line as it curved downhill at a more shallow pitch than the drop-off, and edged nearer the stream. She took her time, watched her steps. It was still dark. She didn't want to fall, or make noise, or mess this up in any way. She wanted to do it right. Stumbling around in the dark would make noise, maybe alert the homeowner-slash-murder suspect.

Her heart beat a little faster.

Zig caught up easily, and her hands were full when she did. She'd taken a beat to grab their flashlights, one of which she handed to Misty, and the disposable camera she'd brought along because they'd left their phones behind. Anyone tracking them wouldn't get farther than their shared dorm room, where the phones were safe in a desk drawer.

It was killing Misty to be without her phone. Out of touch, out of reach.

They'd made their way as close to the stream as the trees provided cover, then crept along its banks in the open, toward a narrow spot. Stones created a bottleneck, where the water ran fast and frothy. Misty took a careful look at her options before she took a running leap and landed on the opposite bank. She turned back to see Zig crossing easily with the help of a large flat rock in the middle. She stepped up beside her, and said, "Work smarter, not harder."

Yeah, she should've seen that handy stepping stone. Maybe she should tamp down her enthusiasm a little bit.

They walked away from the stream, and its gurgling song quieted. Insects whirred their songs on the night air, and Misty thought again how much Eva must have loved living there.

"We'll go to that window first," she said, pointing to the window that was still dark. The one with the moonlight illuminating it was around the corner from it.

"We have to cross open space," Zig said. "Stick to that strip of shadow, from the trees."

"Fast and low," Misty said, nodding. "On three."

Zig rolled her eyes and took off in a running crouch. Misty followed, and then they were hunkering low against the side of the cabin beneath the small, dark window. Misty's heart was pounding. Not from the run. She was in excellent shape, thanks to mermaiding. It was sheer adrenaline that made her blood rush hot through her veins and her skin tingle with awareness. She was having the time of her life.

She turned to face the cabin and rose just enough so that she could see inside. "Holy shit."

Beside her, Zig rose, too.

Inside the small room, illuminated by moonlight flooding in through the opposite window, was a wall entirely covered in small photos, scraps of paper, and news clippings. The photo in the very center was of Eva Quaid. They were too far away to see details of the other photos, but Eva's shot was bigger. There was no spiderweb of string crisscrossing the items, but there were handwritten notes scrawled across several of them.

"We have got to get a closer look at that."

Zig aimed the camera and snapped a shot, but then shook her head. "Not enough light," she whispered. "Maybe we can lighten it up, enlarge it."

"We gotta get inside. Look, there's a computer, too."

"We can't just take it," Zig said.

"I have a flash drive in my pack. If there's anything on there, we can download it."

"We will. When he leaves. Tomorrow."

"What if he doesn't leave?" Misty asked.

Zig grabbed her arm and pulled her down low and a few steps away. "You don't mean we should break in now, while he's there!"

"No." Misty frowned, twisted her lips to one side, mulled for a moment, then said it again, "No, we probably can't do that."

"Probably?"

"But let's come up with a plan to get him out of there just in case. Maybe a fake call from the cops asking him to come down to the station to answer a few new questions... ten years after the fact. Weak, but it might work."

Zig raised her eyebrows and widened her eyes. "Who the hell *are* you?"

RACHEL

The smell of chlorine took me back to swimming lessons with Sandra when we were kids. I was eleven, and entirely blind, sitting on the edge with my feet in the water, and I was overwhelmed by two sensations. The chlorine smell and mind-numbing fear.

I'd been swimming before, lots of times. But I could see then. This was the first summer after I'd gone completely blind. But there was Sandra, my kid sister by a year, standing close enough to touch, only she was *in* the water.

"You don't have to come in," she said. "But everything is exactly the same as when you could see. Promise." She took my hands, but she didn't pull. "We're in the shallow end. You can touch here."

I slid into the water, and it felt good, cool and refreshing against my sun-warmed skin. I was terrified, shaking even, but my sister had me. I trusted her. And as long as she was with me, I knew I'd be okay.

"So, Aunt Rache, you uh, ever seen anything like this before?" Christy asked.

It shook me out of the past and back into the present, where I was standing in a large room with a pool in its center beside my niece, who wanted details about my dream or vision or whatever. She was still wearing her Misty wig. She said that for performances, even Misty wore the wig, tucking her own hair up in a waterproof cap to protect it from the pool chemicals.

"Nothing *just* like this, no," I said.

Beside me, Mason squeezed my hand, like he knew I'd been on a little journey.

I kept looking around. It seemed like a typical indoor pool. Cement apron all the way to the walls, with a door marked LOCKERS on the right side, and another in the center of the rear wall marked EXIT.

Then I saw the *It's a Wonderful Life* retractable pool cover and relived that moment from my vision, when, as a mermaid, I'd bashed my head into an inexplicable ceiling. I felt it again, and my heart contracted with the memory. This had to be the same pool. How many pools had those closing covers over them? And why the hell hadn't they been outlawed? I spotted the control panel for the deadly device near the locker room door— a gray metal box with a lever.

I closed my hand on Mason's upper arm, and his bicep flexed. It was a reflex, he wasn't showing off. He could, but he wasn't. Something about that firm muscle under my hand, grounded me. I took a few steadying breaths. He put his hand over mine.

Two beautiful young women were sitting poolside in swimwear. One had milky white skin and fine, long hair of strawberry blonde with eyebrows to match. The other had dark brown skin and multiple braids that hung halfway down her back. They were both dangling their feet and looking down into the water.

"The pH feels low, to me," one said to the other.

"If that means the water burns your eyes, then yeah," Christy said, and they both turned our way, frowning. Christy cleared her throat, and shifted to Misty voice as she waved a hand our way. "My aunt and uncle," she said, not bothering with our names. "Jasmine and Echo," she said, nodding at each in turn. "Those are their mermaid names."

"Oh, your family's in town," Jasmine said, hopping up to her feet. "No wonder you've been acting so odd."

"Did your twin sister come with them?" Echo asked. I kept thinking how amazing her long braids had been in the water.

You kinda want to stay for the next show, don't you?

Yes, Inner Bitch, I kinda do.

They both came over to where we stood. Echo gave us a nod and a pleasant smile but kept going past us to hit the lever on that gray box. The floor closed over the open tank, pushing a half inch of water ahead of it. Its motor made so much noise I wondered if it could be heard downstairs in the dining room. Closed, it made for a much bigger room and a completely sealed off tank.

"How um... do you breathe down there?" Mason asked. "I saw bubbles coming from some of the plants. Are those—?"

"Yeah, they have air tanks attached by hoses," Christy said. "There's a hidden trigger on the stem."

"Clever," I said. "And the tanks are where?"

"In the control room, off the locker room in back."

"Very cool," I said. "And what happens if the floor gets closed accidentally while a mermaid is still inside? Is there like an escape hatch, or...?"

Christy gave me a wide-eyed stare. Actually, everyone else was looking at me the same way.

"That could never happen," Jasmine said. "There's always someone else here."

"That's a horrifying thought," Echo said, and she rubbed her arms as if she had chills.

"Sorry," I said. "My mind goes to dark places sometimes. Anybody want dessert?"

"Not me," Christy said. "I have plans."

"But we still don't know where your sister is," I reminded her.

She shot a look toward her co-mermaids, then back at me. "*Christy* doesn't want us to know where she is. And it's only for the weekend, Aunt Rache."

"But—"

She held up a hand and kept talking, just like I some-times did when I was on a roll. I wanted to smack her and hug her at the same time. "I'm gonna make a few calls tonight. I know some of her friends. We all hang out when I — when she comes to visit. I'll find out what I can, okay?"

"Something's up with your sister?" Echo asked. "Is there anything we can do, Misty?"

Christy didn't have to make up an answer, because a woman in black spandex and a neon green windbreaker came out of the locker room. She was older than the merfolk, like mid-thirties, lean and tall with gold-blonde hair in a short, layered cut. And she looked *pissed*.

She held up a phone, on which a video of Christy's performance was playing. "What the hell do you call *this*?" she asked Christy.

I stepped in front of my niece, as one does when a barracuda is speeding toward her with blood in its eye. The woman came to a halt and lifted her brows. "And who the hell are you?"

"I'm her aunt. Who the *hell* are you?"

"I'm her coach. Though given what I just saw, she's forgotten everything I ever taught her."

Christy stepped out from behind me and dropped what she probably thought was a calming hand onto my shoulder. "I'm sorry, coach," she said in Misty voice. "I tweaked my back somehow and I'm stiff as hell. I'll do better, I promise." And then with a meaningful look my way, "This job means a lot to me."

The coach's face was no longer angry, but it wasn't friendly either, as it slid my way. "You know this area is staff only."

"Coach Hannah, this is my aunt, Rachel de Luca, and her

96

fiancé, Detective Mason Brown." Was she trying to intimidate the coach using my full name and Mason's cop status?

I nodded hello, offering neither a smile nor a hand.

"Good to meet you," she said, then sent her full attention back to Christy. "I'll go over your routine with you. We can swap in some simplified moves you'll be able to handle." Then she frowned. "You should see a doctor, make sure—"

"It's not that bad," she said quickly. "And thanks, I'd appreciate some easier—"

"You two," the coach said. She'd said what she'd wanted to Christy (who she thought was really Misty) and turned her entire focus to Jasmine and Echo. "Where the hell is Toby?"

"Running late," Jasmine said. "Again."

"Well, he'd better get here soon. Who the hell closed the pool? We have work to do!" She clapped her hands twice so sharply I jumped. Then she walked over to the wall and pulled the lever. The cover growled open. "Let's go, next show's in an hour!"

Jasmine and Echo ran into the locker room with the coach right on their heels. "I'll be right in," Christy called. Then her voice dropped an octave, and her innocent round eyes went cat as she turned to Mason and me. "I'll call her friends after my shift. Promise."

"Or you can just give me their contact info, and Mace and I can—"

"Invade my sister's privacy," she finished. "She's not missing. She just wants a weekend alone. You guys staying in town?"

"Yeah," Mason said. "I got us a place." His eyes shifted to

mine, and there was a sparkle in there. He had something up his sleeve, something he was a little bit excited about.

I said to Christy, "Okay. Do it your way. Call us the minute you find out anything."

"I'll call you in the morning," she said.

I rolled my eyes. "I'll be up at six."

"I'll be up at ten," she countered. But then she smiled a little. "Just kidding. I'll call you at eight."

"Good visit."

She hugged me goodbye, the brat. "You can go out this door." She walked as she talked, pushed the big exit door open and held it. Beyond was a two-level metal stairway with a landing in between. It only had a railing on one side.

"Be careful, you guys. It's a long way down."

"Did she just call us old?" I asked as I stepped through the door she held.

"She would never," Mason replied, sending a wink back at Christy. "Now hold onto the railing, dear. I don't want you to break a hip."

Christy backed inside and let the door close, and we continued to descend. The staircase rattled like metallic hell with every step, but it felt solid enough. "That one side being open has to be some kind of code violation, doesn't it?" I asked.

Mason nodded. "Probably. You want me to go back in and arrest someone for it?"

"No," I said, and I laughed. Then I stopped laughing. "Not yet."

CHAPTER 6

RACHEL

"You didn't book us a hotel room, did you?" I asked as Mason drove through the countryside. I could tell he was up to something by the poorly contained excitement on his handsome face, despite the concern in his eyes. He hadn't shaved this morning, and his scruff was at that perfect point that made it all but impossible for me to keep my hands off him.

"Nope."

"What *did* you book us?"

He looked sideways at me and wiggled his eyebrows. "That." He pointed, but all I saw was somebody's house. A pretty stunning house, actually. Asymmetrical, dark wood and glass, wrap-around deck, lawn out of an HGTV show, and as he pulled farther along the curving driveway, I glimpsed what looked like a flower garden out back beyond a little gate.

"Is it some kind of B and B?" I asked.

"Yeah, the Air kind. We have the whole place for the weekend, with the option to extend through Thursday. Fully stocked. Anything we find inside is for our use." He shut off the car and got out.

I loved the place at first sight. "It's big enough for the whole family," I said when he punched the combination into the door lock to let us in. There was a wide-open floor plan, with a hardwood counter between living room and eat-in kitchen. There was a brown sofa with a pair of recliners in darker brown and mustard. They looked cozy and clean.

"Four bedrooms upstairs," Mason said. "The master is through here."

"How do you know all that?" I asked.

"Online tour. Come on." We crossed the living room and entered a short hallway. There was one door on the left, one on the right. I opened the right first and peeked in to see a big room with a treadmill, stationary bike, and weight bench. There was a TV mounted to one wall, and windows all around with views of that garden in back; a haze of pink and yellow, violet and red, with splashes of deep purple here and there and paths in between.

We backed out and stepped into the master bedroom. A gigantic maple sleigh bed took up most of the room. It seemed like a marshmallow cloud with its fluffy white duvet and pillow covers. Two dressers, walk-in closet, attached bathroom, but best of all were the sliding glass doors out onto the deck. "There's a hot tub in that garden," I said, pointing.

"Guaranteed freshly drained, sanitized, and refilled," he said. "And exactly what my back needs after all that driving."

"I'm gonna hit the shower first," I said. "Keep the water warm for me." I grabbed the front of his shirt and pulled him in for a kiss. "This is amazing. Thank you."

"*De nada*," he replied.

So I hopped into the big shower— not as big as mine, but whose was?— and I thought. I thought a lot. This was way nicer than a hotel. He was trying to make it special. Not that he needed to. Every day with Mason was special. I adored the man.

But I'd been slow about picking our next wedding date. We'd picked three wedding dates already, but Covid had other ideas. After the third pandemic spike, we'd put it off indefinitely.

And now I couldn't shake that dream.

Maybe my hesitance had made my hot cop a little bit insecure. I should feel mean and want to make that right, and I did, but I also felt high as a kite that he loved me that much. I mean, I knew he did, but still, having it be that front and center, so big he'd get nervous...

Didn't he know he was the only guy in the entire world for me?

I went back outside wearing a towel. Mason was already in there with a dewy can of beer in his hand. I slid into delicious heat, losing the towel and most of the air in my lungs on the way. "*So* nice," I moaned, sinking all the way to my ears. Mason laughed, a low, sexy laugh and I knew what he was thinking, and curled my toes against his foot.

"Your drink is behind you."

I looked, and there in a cup-sized depression was a dewy glass with dark liquid and two ice cubes. I took it and sipped, then made a face. "That's not Diet Coke."

"It's Diet *Cola*," he said. "Says so on the can."

"Ahh. Yet the beer has a name."

"And unlike the teeny tiny bottle I added to your *cola*, it's full-size."

"I guess you rate." I held out my glass, and he tinked his can against it. I was sitting across from him, but our legs were together under the water, calves moving gently against each other now and then like languishing lovers.

I sipped my drink and waited for it to kick in. It took way less than it used to. We hardly ever drank at home anymore.

The second he'd turned twenty-one, Jeremy had applied to the police academy. Nine months later, he was a rookie cop in the Broome County Sheriff's department. The reduction in our booze intake was probably good for both of us.

But when we were away, we indulged in a nip or two.

"This is nice, this place," I said. "There's room for Myrtle, even."

"I miss her, too."

"It's weird not having her here."

"I know."

"I'm worried about those fugue states," I said. "She seems so normal, other than that. Well, that and her independent streak."

"We'll hear from the vet soon. All those tests he ran, he'll find out what's up with her. He's good at his job."

"By Monday. That's what he said." I hated waiting. My entire life I'd hated waiting. I wanted everything *now*. I'd always wanted everything now. I'd wanted to marry Mason *now*. Three times and counting.

Maybe once we figured this out. Maybe once we found Misty and knew she was safe.

"What do you think Misty is up to? "What's your stuff telling you?"

I took another sip, then sank back into the water. The heat was relaxing my muscles and mind. "I think the mermaid dream has to mean something. It would be a helluva coincidence for me to dream about a mermaid in trouble, then find out Misty's working as one. And now so is Christy. Not very well, but she's working as one."

He listened. There was a pause before he answered. When we'd first started seeing each other, those long pauses had made me wonder if he was listening to me. I knew now that they meant he was listening intently and thinking about his reply.

"When there's something you need to know," he said at length, "these ride-along dreams, where you're inside someone else's experience, are the way you find out. They're the way whoever or whatever is out there, tells you. God, or the Universe or—"

"Or your brother," I said. I didn't have this "gift" until Mason's dead brother's corneas had restored my eyesight.

"Somebody is trying to tell you something," he said.

I nodded, went for another sip, and found my glass empty.

"I got you, babe." Mason slid out of the water and went over the side.

"Water this time," I called.

In less than a minute he was back in the water, handing me a fresh glass of water with a lemon wedge and a few ice cubes.

I slid around the tub until I was right up against him with a jet pulsing into the small of my back, easing more of my worry knots. "I feel the message is that one of the girls is in trouble," I said.

"Or maybe the message is that a *mermaid* is in trouble," he suggested.

"Oh." My muscles unclenched a little more and it was more than just the hot tub. "Oh, that might be it. Maybe it's not Misty or Charity, but someone they work with. But what did that have to do with our wedding? Why did the twins drown at our wedding?"

"You said the wedding dream—"

"Nightmare."

"—was different. Not a ride-along. Maybe not even part of your stuff. Maybe just a normal, garden-variety nightmare. Nerves."

I considered that. "I guess after planning and cancelling three times—"

"To keep people from getting sick and maybe dying due to an exposure at our pandemic-era wedding."

"People dying... because of our wedding." I repeated it slowly.

"The twins have asthma," he reminded me unnecessarily.

It was true, and while it hadn't been an issue for either of them in years, we'd been terrified what would happen if they got Covid. Sandra had been so vigilant neither of them had caught it, even when she and Jim had. They'd made the girls move in with us for those two weeks during their senior year.

"We *have* spent a lot of energy trying to keep them from getting sick," I said, nodding.

"See?" Mason asked. "And maybe your stuff picked up on the girls' keeping this mermaid thing a secret, and tangled that up with the nightmare to create the mermaid dream."

I nodded slowly. "That... that might be it."

"That might be it," Mason agreed. "So, we find Misty, just in case. And we should account for all the other mermaids, as well."

"Yeah. I'll talk to them, see if they've noticed anything odd at work." I leaned my head onto his shoulder. "But our top priority is to locate Misty. I don't like not knowing for sure she's okay."

"I agree," he said. "And Christy said she'd make a few calls. I bet she'll have something for us by morning."

His logic and his... wonderfulness eased the tension from my mind as surely as the hot water was easing it from my body. This was nice, I decided. The hot water, the garden's floral perfume, and Mason so close and so attentive. The man adored me.

He pulled me closer, bending his head for a soft kiss, then settling himself lower on the seat, so the water covered his shoulders.

It was a beautiful night.

Until my cellphone pinged. I reached for it with a wet hand.

Christy: Check this Out.

There was a link called *Zig Tales,* with a preview showing. Frowning, I tapped. Mason was close enough to see everything I did. *Zig Tales*, it turned out, was a podcast. There were two seasons. Season 1: Dog Gone. 10 Episodes. Its thumbnail had a cover-model Yorkie with "SOLVED" stamped across its shaggy Ewok face. And then where was Season 2, where the thumbnail was a brunette mermaid with a tail that was powder blue at the waist, darkening gradually to darkest blue at the tail. The tail fin and "scales" were edged in silver that caught the light. Her long, dark curls trailed behind her in the water. She wasn't facing the camera but gazing ahead with an unnamed yearning in her eyes.

"*'The Missing Mermaid'*." Mason read the title like he couldn't believe it.

"That's her." My words emerged in a croak. "That's the mermaid from my vision." In my mind's eye, I saw her again, sinking to the bottom of that pool like a leaf floating from an autumn tree. Her hair had trailed upward as she'd fallen, and so had the trickle of blood from her head.

"Are you sure?" He took the phone from my hand, probably because he knew I was going to drop it into the hot tub if he didn't. His arm was around my shoulders, and he was watching my face with a look in his eyes that said "I'm worried" and "I've got you" and "I love you" all at once.

"I'm sure. And that means she's real. That means it was a real ride-along. And that means... the mermaid is probably dead."

He closed his eyes slowly, then frowned and tapped the phone back to Messages when a new one popped up.

Christy: Zig is Misty's roommate.

My brain finally made the connection that had been sparking since I'd seen the name. I snatched the phone back from Mason.

Rachel: Right! Karen Ziglar, the aspiring mystery writer.

Christy: Mystery podcaster. The future is digital, Aunt Rache. She started it last year. Remember Misty telling us about it?

Rachel: I do now.

Christy: Listen to the second season. There are only three episodes. Text me after.

Rachel: They're long. We'll text you in the morning.

Christy: After. Also, just so you know, I've filled Jere in on all this.

I hesitated, met Mason's eyes.

Rachel: You're worried too?

Christy: You had a mermaid dream or vision or something. Her roomie is investigating a missing mermaid. Yes. I'm worried.

Rachel: I should text your mom.

> Christy: Not THAT worried. Don't terrify her until there's a reason. Misty said she'd only be gone through the weekend.

I sighed. Mason said, "There's nothing we can do tonight, I think. In the morning, I'll visit the local PD. Talk to the detective in charge of the case."

I nodded and texted.

> Rachel: Mason will visit PD tomorrow. Let us know if you hear anything more.

> Christy: I'd feel it if she wasn't okay. So she must be okay.

> Rachel: I agree. She must be fine. Try to get some sleep.

> Christy: Night, Aunt Rache.

I frowned and looked at Mason, then I tapped the play button on Episode 1, *Fathomless*, propped the phone against my dewy glass, and sank a little deeper into the hot, bubbling water to listen.

ZIG TALES

This is Zig-Tales. We solve mysteries here.
Welcome to Season Two, The Missing Mermaid.

THE MERMAID MURDER

I wanted to call it The Mermaid Murder, but that's the thing with this case. We don't know for sure there was a murder. What we do know is that ten years ago this very week, a beautiful mermaid vanished, and she hasn't been seen again since.

Shy, beautiful, twenty-seven-year-old Eva Quaid was the star at a club in Saratoga Springs, New York, where she performed as a professional mermaid. Yes, people, that's a thing. She wore a blue silicone mermaid tail and a faux seashell bikini top, and her skin always glittered when she turned in the lights.

Her mermaid name was Esmeralda, and she was magical.

So was her life. She'd been a mermaid for several years. But that last year was special, because she fell in love with Paul Quaid, a metalwork artist who'd stopped in one night to see the show. He would later say that the minute he saw her, he knew. She must've known too, because they were married within six months, and Eva was living happily with Paul in a woodland log cabin twenty miles north of the Springs. Eva waited tables by day, and performed as a mermaid on weekends— nightly, during summer and early autumn, when the tourists poured in. Paul cut and welded woodland creatures in his little workshop beside their rustic cabin, with a stream running by. It was an idyllic existence.

Until one weekend.

Paul was away at an art show, one he'd attended every single year for the past five and has attended every year since. The show provided a good chunk of his annual revenue, and he never missed it. Eva left her cabin with her mermaid tail in its carrying case, heading, we presume, for the pool at the club to practice for an important show. The owners were in town, and she wanted to impress them.

At least, that was what she texted to Paul. It was six a.m.

when those texts were sent. They were the last ones she ever sent; the last communication between Eva Quaid and anyone living.

Her car would be found much later, abandoned along a deserted stretch of road between her home and the club. Apparently she never got there. Eva's handbag, cash, credit cards, and cell phone were all still in the car.

But Eva, and her mermaid tail, too, were missing.

What followed was an intense investigation by the Saratoga Springs Police Department, with cooperation from the County Sheriff's Department and even the State Troopers. Detective Jen Scott, a former Army explosives ordinance expert, was in charge of the case. According to the papers from the time, everyone who worked at the club was questioned, including its three owners, known to staff as 'the billionaire bad boys'; a trio of unrelated men whose fathers gave them the funds to buy the place. Eva's new husband, artist Paul Quaid, was also questioned no less than three times. Police had also interrogated the club's bartender, Earl Mackey, who had a tense relationship with Eva, according to their co-workers. We have information that things might have been a little more complicated than that. But everyone had alibis, and none of detective-in-charge Jen Scott's leads panned out. And now, ten years later, her case remains unsolved.

Here at Zig Tales, we intend to remedy that. We have resources that SSPD's decade-old investigation didn't have. And unlike them, this case will be our only focus until we solve it.

And trust me, we will solve it.

So hit that subscribe button and then share this podcast with every mystery-lover, Springs resident, and mermaid fan you know, as Zig Tales takes on the case of The Missing Mermaid.

RACHEL

"Holy shit," I said, three hours later. Each episode had run a full hour, but a lot of that time was clever, compelling filler. Anecdotes about Eva from her childhood, offered by school mates; other memories from people who'd worked with her at the diner. It was all too compelling to fast-forward through.

Zig read off a mini bio of each of the original suspects, along with that suspect's alibi, then made several attempts to poke holes in it. She claimed she had even driven routes with a timer, but she had yet to find any real bombshells.

Mason nodded as the final episode ended. And then he said, "Misty's helping her."

"Misty wrote the scripts," I replied. He looked at me oddly, and I said, "What? It's her voice. I recognize it. It's a lot like mine."

"Okay. I was basing my conclusion on it being way too coincidental that she's working as a mermaid—"

"At the same club—" I added.

"While rooming with the podcaster." He concluded my thought.

"My God, Mason, do you think she's inherited your crime-solving gene?"

"I'm not her blood uncle."

"No shit. She got it by osmosis."

"Or she got it from you."

I opened my mouth to deny I was any kind of sleuth, but then lifted my brows, tipped my head to one side, and considered his point. I had, in fact, helped to solve several crimes. Mostly as a way of surviving them, but still. "That might be true."

We'd left the hot tub behind halfway through the first episode, gone inside, dried off and changed, then continued listening on the cozy sofa. The electric fireplace was warm and soothing. The owner had left us each a giant, homemade chocolate chip cookie, which we ate with freshly brewed decaf, since it was late.

Episode 1: *Fathomless,* set up the story, giving the background and introducing the cast of characters. Episode 2: *The Depths*, followed the whereabouts of Eva Quaid's husband Paul on the weekend she'd vanished. It revealed juicy morsels like the $100K life insurance policies Eva and Paul had taken out, each for the other, just in case, and the fact that Paul's art brought in barely enough to scrape by. Since the marriage, his standard of living had improved in small, but meaningful ways. His rustic cabin soon had things like Satellite TV, air conditioning, and a paid-up electric bill. Two incomes were always better than one.

The show did a great job planting nuggets of suspicion about the husband, only to reveal that there were hotel surveillance videos and footage of the art show showing Paul, right where he said he'd been, at the time of his bride's disappearance. "At this time," Zig had said in her dulcet tones, "we have not seen this footage ourselves, and the FOIA forms we've filed with the local authorities are apparently being slow-walked through a red-tape jungle."

"Misty's roomie is good at this," I said. "She really has something here." We were wearing our plush, matching spa robes— I know, it makes me gag too!— sipping our decaf, still nibbling on the cookies.

"We should talk to this Zig person," Mason said. "If anyone knows where Misty is, it's her."

I nodded and tapped my phone. 12:13 a.m. lit up in white across the screen. Then I called Christy. It took her three rings to answer, and she sounded sleepy. "We listened. And we need to talk to Zig."

"No shit," she said. "Like I wouldn't have thought of that."

"Grumpy much?"

"Sorry. I don't wake up cheerful like you, Aunt Rache."

We both knew damn well that late night or early morning calls caused me to wake up like a bear with a toothache, but I wasn't going to acknowledge that. "So, you talked to her, then?"

"Can't find her. She's not responding to texts or even reading them. Calls go straight to voicemail. I'm betting they're together."

"Great," Mason said. "Veronica Mars times two."

"Who the fuck is Veronica Mars?" Christy asked.

Mason mouthed "ouch" but didn't say it out loud.

"We've got to figure out where they went," I said.

"In the morning, though," Christy replied. "We can't do anything on no sleep. Besides, I don't think she's in trouble. I think I'd know if she was in trouble."

"I don't feel like she's in trouble either," I said. But my

vision or whatever sure suggested she was heading for it. And I had to intervene before she arrived.

"Good then," Christy said. "Let's talk in the morning, all right?"

"Yeah. Okay. Good night, Christy. Thanks for the help."

"Night."

I disconnected and turned to Mason. "I don't think Misty is with another guy at all. I think she's investigating the missing mermaid with her podcaster pal Zig."

"I admit I like that theory a lot better," Mason said. "At least until I get to the part where investigating a crime can be dangerous."

I nodded in full agreement.

"But then why did she dump Jeremy?" Mason asked.

"She didn't dump him. They're on a break." I blinked, but no reason came to mind. "We should let him know, don't you think? Because he's probably jumped to the same conclusion we did, and—"

"I'll call him first thing in the morning." Mason took my phone from my hand, put his hands on my shoulders and pulled me to my feet. "But in the meantime, how about we test out that gigantic bed in the master?"

I took a big breath and harnessed my racing thoughts. Then I took another one and let some of the tension out of my body with it. "You got us this big, romantic place for the weekend and I'm not properly appreciating it, am I?"

"You're worried about your nieces."

"I crimed away our entire hot tub time," I said. "But don't worry, babe. I'll make it up to you." I slid my arms around his neck.

He wrapped his around my waist and pulled me close, lowered his head and growled a playful little growl. Then he kissed me like he'd just returned from a year fighting Nazis overseas. Oh, *hell* yes.

Beep! Beep!

The blast of a car horn made me jump so hard I smacked my forehead into Mason's nose. "What the—?"

One arm still around me, Mason went to the front door and opened it to see who the hell was blasting their horn in the driveway of our romantic hideaway in the middle of the night.

Jeremy. Who else?

I scowled at him hard enough to melt his tires. But then he got out of the car, went around to the passenger side, opened up the door, and scooped out a sixty-pound English bulldog and I went soft and gooey.

"Myrtle!" I said, pushing past Mason, out the door, and down the driveway. I leaned in and kissed her face. She smiled from ear to ear, (yes, dogs *do* smile,) snarfed in joy, and squirmed in his arms so hard she farted.

Myrtle hated being carried with the fires of a thousand hells, with two specific exceptions: up or down our stairs, by Mason.

Jere hunkered and set her down. I crouched and she shot right to me almost as if she could see me there. Her other senses were sharper than ever before, I thought as I scratched her face and rubbed her ears the way she loved best. She wiggled to tell me she'd missed me. "Okay, okay," I said. "I know, I missed you too."

I rose and hugged Jeremy. "Why are you here?"

"You find Misty yet?"

"How do you even know she's not here?"

"Dorm room is empty, and her car's gone. Plus, Christy called and spilled her guts a few hours ago. Myrt and I left right away."

"I don't think it's that dire."

"Christy says you're worried. If you're worried, I'm worried. That's why I'm here. By the way, Myrt's favorite bed, feeding dishes, and chew toys are in the trunk. I should—"

"I'll grab them," Mason said, and took the keys.

Jeremy was a good man, I thought. A lot like his uncle. Even thinking he'd been dumped— which he hadn't— he'd come all the way out here to help us look for Misty. He was worried.

I was, too.

"We're pretty sure she's helping her podcaster friend Zig investigate a cold case. Come on inside, and we'll fill you in. Then we're gonna get some sleep while you listen to a couple hours' worth of podcasts to get caught up."

"I listened on the way out," he said. "And I think I'm all caught up. Where do we start looking?"

I opened the door and held it for Jeremy to go inside, then for Mason, whose arms were full of Myrt's luggage. After Jere was out of earshot, Mason murmured near my ear, "His timing could've been better." And his warm breath sent a delicious shiver right down my spine.

"Yeah, but he brought Myrt," I said. "You think that's gonna be all right with the owners?"

"It's Myrt," he said. "She'll spend most of her time on her bed. They'll never even know she's been here."

"Maybe not. Providing we vacuum all her little white hairs before we leave." Then I kissed his chin and took my dog inside to show her around our temporary home away from home.

CHAPTER 7

CHRISTY

When Christy arrived at The Sapphire club at a quarter to sunup, there were other cars in the lot. She figured maybe cleaning staff or something. She took Misty's tail, safe inside its bag, from the back of her little car, hauled it over her shoulder, and headed up the two flights of exterior metal stairs, clanging and banging all the way, then through the rear entrance into the pool room.

It wasn't empty, as she'd expected at this ungodly hour. She dropped the bag across a bench, unsure what to do. Echo was there, and Jasmine, and orange-haired Toby, the only guy in the bunch. Two tails had assumed the position, out of their bags and laid out on the floor with their zippers pulled all the way down.

"Well, come on, we've been waiting," Echo said. "You bring your tail?"

"Yeah. Um..." Christy stood there not sure what to do. This smacked of an intervention or something— probably *or something*. They still thought she was the good twin.

Didn't they?

She walked past them and into the locker room, put her stuff into her locker, changed into her swimsuit— not the glittering clamshell bikini top that went with the tail, but just a simple black tank suit. She picked up her tail as she passed on her way to the pool, then laid it out on the floor the way the others all were.

Donning the tail without help was difficult. Christy wasn't sure how she'd even thought she'd be able to practice alone. But the whole school of fish had shown up.

"So, before we get started, we should probably introduce ourselves, since we never did that," Jasmine said, with a steady, serious look in her pale blue eyes.

The bottom fell out of Christy's stomach.

"We know you're not Misty," she went on, "and we know she has a twin sister. So?"

"We're not going to rat you out," Toby added, "even though she abandoned us without warning. She'd get fired if we did."

Echo nodded. "Right, and if you don't get better at this fast, there's no way you're gonna fool Mackey, much less Coach Hannah, so... we came to help."

"We'll give you some pointers," Toby said. "A few tips, a couple of easy tricks, not a real workout. Not when we're performing tonight."

Christy looked at each of them in turn. The coach had told her which moves to cut and which to keep in, but what the merfolk were suggesting was actual help. "Shit, you guys are amazing people, aren't you?"

"Yeah, we are," Echo said.

"We freaking rock!" Toby raised rock fingers to the sky.

She heaved a sigh, then said, "I'm Christy, Misty's twin sister. It's nice to actually meet you." Then she dropped onto all fours atop her unzipped tail, slid her feet and lower legs into place and adjusted the uppermost edge at her waist.

Jasmine came and stood over her head, facing her feet, grabbed the long cord attached to the tail's zipper, and began to pull it up. The farther it went, the harder it was to pull, because it fit like a second skin, which was the whole point.

With her zipper zipped, she rolled sideways and right over the edge into the pool. The water was cool, not cold. No shock on contact, which she appreciated. Moments later, the rest of the merfolk joined her.

Echo said, "You kept closing your eyes yesterday. You have to keep them open, and you have to be smiling any time you face the audience."

"Okay."

"When you need a breath," Jasmine said, "pretend to smell one of the flower bubblers. Cup it with your forward hand, to hold the petals up, so when you close your lips around the mouthpiece to breathe, it's completely hidden."

"Otherwise," said Toby, "It destroys the illusion."

They were floating in a loose circle. The slightest motion of their downward aimed tails was enough to keep them afloat. Their hands were in constant motion to keep them upright. "Now, in today's show, I'm Prince Eric. There will be a video clip from *The Little Mermaid* playing on the front of the tank. There's a storm and Prince Eric is swept overboard. Then, the video shuts off, the lights come up in the tank. I fall into the water and you, Misty— er, Christy—"

"Call me Misty. Preserve the illusion for the few people who don't already know," Christy said.

"Got it. Misty, you come out from behind the rocks. Echo and Jasmine are trying to steer you away from me, but you save me. We kiss, and you carry me to the surface."

Toby continued, moving his hands in the air as if he were seeing the story play out there. "Then the screen comes back up to show Eric waking on the beach, confused. He dives back into the water to find the mermaid who saved him. Cut back to the tank. You know the rest. You've read the script, right?"

"Yeah." Sappiest shit she'd ever seen. "My thought is, it would be better if one of you took the lead role, though. I'm no good at this."

Echo shook her head. "It won't work. Mackey would want to know why. Your sister's been begging for the lead. I can't believe she would take off on a weekend with a show."

"It's not like it's opening night," Jasmine said.

"So, you ready to rehearse?" Toby asked. "And listen, I know it's weird, but you don't have to worry about the kiss. I'm *totally* gay."

"No!" Christy said, touching her chest with one hand. She winked at Toby, who usually had glitter on his cheeks and the coolest little silicone gills glued to either side of his neck. He grinned at her teasing. He was just in baggy swim trunks today, since he'd be playing a human in their little skit.

"Just follow our lead," Jasmine said, and she did this weird thing with her breaths, taking three really long deep ones right in a row. "It builds up your oxygen," Toby explained. "You'll see."

So she did what Jasmine had done, and so did Echo and they dove down together.

Echo turned to look at her and pointed to her own eyes and smiling mouth.

Christy opened her eyes wider, smiled as bright as Ariel herself, and received a thumbs-up. Then Jasmine swam over, and did a "watch this" sign, pointing two fingers at Christy's eyes, then one at herself. With a sweep of her tail, she propelled herself into a long, loose somersault. Then she pointed at Christy, who imitated the move once, then had to flip down to a flower for a breath. When she came back, Jasmine clasped her forearms and moved them in just the way she wanted. Then nodded at her to try again, with a slow-down motion, pumping her palms downward.

This time, Christy flipped her tail, propelling herself downward, and then she turned a full somersault beautifully — or it felt beautiful to her, all graceful and elegant as if in slow motion— without pinwheeling her arms like a child in a backyard pool.

Hell, she had to breathe again. She swam to a flower. The others hadn't had to do so once. Echo pointed to herself, then performed a perfect a kind of whirlwind pirouette, descending like a corkscrew all the way to the bottom. Then with one powerful swoosh of her tail, she propelled herself upward again. This time, she repeated the move in slow motion, demonstrating the undulation that began at her waist, and carried all the way to her tail, and the way she held her arms to assist her in the spin.

Christy nodded, but she couldn't take it anymore. She flexed her abs to move her hips and legs as one. It took every muscle in her body to move that tail through the water. Her sister must have abs like rocks if she'd been doing this for long. Her head broke the surface, and she took a great big open-mouthed breath and felt a little dizzy.

The others popped up one by one all around her. "It's okay. Just rest a minute," Echo said.

"Yeah. But I want to try that corkscrew move. I just need a sec." Christy leaned on the edge of the pool and let her tail hang still.

"That was a great somersault, for someone who's never done it before," Toby said.

"Never done it like that, at least" she replied. "I didn't even know professional mermaids were a thing until now."

"We're catching on. There's a Netflix series."

"I'm amazed. So is this something new, or am I just oblivious?"

"It's been around for decades," Jasmine said.

Then Echo said, "Wait, you only showed up yesterday for Misty's shift. You haven't seen the gallery yet!"

"The gallery?"

"Every mermaid who ever swam here has a photo in the banquet room, the one they reserve for private parties, with a full side view of the tank all to themselves."

"When there's someone in there, we angle everything

slightly that way, and play up to them. It costs a lot of money to book that room."

"I heard it was booked tonight," Echo said in her whisper-soft voice.

"I'd know if it was." Jasmine pressed herself up out of the water with her strong arms, then half turned to get her butt up there, but she couldn't really bend in the middle very much. She flipped herself facedown on the concrete and said, "Toby, come unzip me. I'll call Mackey and find out what's up."

Echo said, "Come on, Christy, let's try the spiral." She took a couple of breaths, then let herself sink, and Christy followed.

RACHEL

Mason, Myrtle, and I slept right up until my phone played the opening riff from *Barracuda*, the custom ringtone I'd set for Christy. Misty's was Elton John's *Blue Eyes*.

Maybe I was going to have to rethink hers.

I picked it up. 8:14 a.m. Mason pulled his pillow over his head. I put the phone on speaker though, because I knew he wouldn't want me to suffer from sleeplessness alone.

"Morning, Aunt Rache." It was Christy and she sounded suspiciously upbeat. "Wanna meet for breakfast?"

Mason moved the pillow and picked up his head. His face

had pillow lines and his hair was an angry brown chicken. He said, "I could eat."

"Why don't you come here?" I asked. "The place is stocked. I saw some pumpkin bagels in the fridge. Jeremy's upstairs anyway, and—"

"It doesn't sound like you're at a hotel."

"No, Mason got us a house-share for the weekend."

"Sounds romantic."

It was for a minute. Inner Bitch said what I was thinking but not saying myself. (That's what Inner Bitch always does, come to think of it.)

"Doesn't matter," Christy said. "You should come to me."

"But why?" I moaned.

"Because the club is empty, and I have a borrowed key and I might've found a clue."

"Okay. How long should the place be empty?"

"Two hours, so hurry your asses up."

I flung back the covers and got up. "We'll be there ASAP."

My bulldog moaned as if she knew that meant she had to wake up, too. So did my cop, but his was more playful. He got up, pulled on a Terry robe. "I'll wake Jere."

We took high speed showers, both vehicles, and the dog. Jeremy wanted to drive himself in case we needed to split up after. He and his Firebird followed us right into the closest fast food-drive-through, where I ordered massive quantities of caffeine and empty calories. About halfway through the still-too-hot cuppa Joe, I sort of blinked into awareness of the world around me.

Mason was driving. He'd devoured his McBreakfast and was nursing his java. He was starting to come more fully online after only three hours of sleep. Oh, he could snap to full on, sharp-as-a-tack super cop mode in 0.3 seconds, if necessary. But until it became necessary, he tended to take his time. He and Myrtle had that in common.

She was sitting in the center of the back seat, with her doggy-seat belt harness in place. She was right in the opening between our bucket seats and wore a big smile. There were few things she loved more than riding in the car. I reached back and pet her head, and she rubbed against my hand.

"I haven't told Christy any details about that dream," I said completely out of context when we pulled into the club's driveway.

I could imagine the mechanisms in Mason's brain cranking to life, connections firing in search of meaning, finding it. "Are you going to?"

"Only if I think she needs to know."

Christy was waiting outside the front doors when we pulled up, and she waved us around to the back of the building. Jeremy followed us around in his car.

"Like we wouldn't have thought to put the cars out of sight," I muttered.

"Yeah," Mason said, because he was always on my side.

We parked and got out. I unbuckled Myrtle, kissed her face, and unwrapped a fresh, long-lasting chewy treat from the glove compartment where I always kept a few. She'd nosh on that treat the entire time we were gone. The car was in the shade, and we left two windows cracked for a fresh breeze. It was cool enough that the A.C. wasn't necessary.

Jeremy got out of his car and came to join the huddle, hands in his pockets, not saying much.

"Hey Jere," Christy said, and she gave him a sisterly hug. "How are you doing? You okay?"

He shrugged one shoulder. "I'm fine. It's fine."

"It's not. But for what it's worth, I don't think it's about you."

He met my eyes briefly, because that was word for word what I'd said, and I knew he disagreed.

Christy was wearing leggings and an oversized hoodie with The Sapphire Club's stained-glass mermaid windows on the front. Her short dark hair was wet, and she smelled of chlorine.

"You've been in the pool already?" I asked when I hugged her hello.

"I came in early to practice. The others were here waiting. They knew I wasn't Misty, and they knew she had a twin, so they called me on it."

"Shit," I said.

"Is she in trouble?" Jere asked.

Christy shook her head left and right. "I don't think so. They said they wouldn't rat us out, and they showed me some moves so I can hold my own today. Mr. Mackey told Echo the private room is booked. That means there are VIPs coming tonight.

"VIPs, huh?" Mason asked. "Like who? Moby Dick? Nemo? Mr. Limpet?" He grinned at his own humor. I snort-laughed and smacked his shoulder in appreciation. We found each other hilarious.

"Who the fuck is Mr. Limpet?" Christy asked.

Jeremy shrugged. "Damned if I know."

Mason opened his arms toward me and said, "You see?"

"I know. I know, baby. We tried. They grew up before we could force feed them every classic."

"Antique." Christy coughed the word as if to disguise it, but not really, and it made Jeremy smile a little bit, which I thought had been the whole idea.

"*The Incredible Mr. Limpet*," I said. "Google it. Meanwhile, let's see this clue you dragged us out of bed for."

"You got it." We followed her up the noisy metal staircase to the reinforced steel door, where Christy inserted a key. She led us into the pool room, with its chlorine-scented, too-warm air. The pool lights were off, and the water looked dark. I hadn't seen the phantom mermaid again and was rather surprised she wasn't jumping at the opportunity to appear and splash water into my face. Maybe she didn't need to. Maybe I was doing what she wanted me to do.

Christy crossed the room, went through a door with a much nicer staircase, and down to the dining room where chairs were up on tables and the floor gleamed under a fresh shine. The curtains were drawn over the front of the mermaid tank.

The place was dark. It had only a few windows, and those bore light-blocking shades hiding behind sheer blue curtains. I imagined sunlight reflecting off the glass tank would mess with the audience's ability to see the mermaids inside.

We didn't step into the main restaurant though, just entered a door at the end of it. "This is the private party room," Christy said. "There are photos of every mermaid who ever performed here."

The room had its own little bar and soft leather chairs mounted to the floor around small tables, a sectional sofa took up two walls, and it looked as if every seat reclined.

The fourth wall was glass, the end of the mermaid tank, but the other three were lined in photos; rows of them in matching frames, perfectly spaced. Every shot was a mermaid in some enchanting full-body pose, eyes open, smile wide, tail glittering. Underneath was a first name— the mermaid name, anyway— followed by a favorite quote or thought.

There was a shot of Misty floating with her tail curled up around behind her, her hair like cornsilk tendrils in the clear water. Not a wig, I was sure of it. Not for the photo. The plate underneath read; Misty; still in search of her catchphrase.

"She didn't use a mermaid name," Christy said. "Said she couldn't have come up with one better for it than her own. I concur, by the way."

There was Echo, dark as night in her pristine white-and-silver tail. And next was Jasmine, pale as a milk, with a black tail that flashed purple when the light hit it at the right angle. Then came Toby with his orange hair in tall spikes all over his head. His flame-red and neon-orange tail looked like pure fire. "Let it be" was his quote.

And the parade continued. "There must be a fifty of them," I said, moving slowly around the room as the shots grew progressively older. You could tell the photos' age by the hair, makeup, and amount of skin covered. Also, by the quality of the tails and of the photos themselves. But what a collection of beautiful people, mostly women, a handful of men, floating and twirling, or basking on beaches or rocks. Their tails were every shade in existence. The sayings underneath had been a recent addition. More and more just had their names.

I walked slowly around the room, taking in every single photo. I wanted to feel them, in that way I sometimes could, but I would have to close my eyes and I couldn't. It was like something out of a fantasy, this gallery of mermaids.

And then she was there. The tag on the frame said Esmeralda, but the face was the same one in my dream.

"This is her," I said. "The mermaid from my vision. And the one from the podcast." I pressed my fingertips to the glass over her face, and then thinking fast, I snapped a photo of the photo with my phone. "According to the podcast, Esmeralda was her mermaid name." Beneath her name were the words, "Under the sea, where I long to be."

"How odd," Christy said. "I wonder why the podcast didn't mention her rather dark catch phrase?"

"Probably saving it for the next episode," Mason said.

"The next episode," Jeremy said slowly. "You know they've been checking on the whereabouts of the people who knew and worked with Eva Quaid. Maybe that's where Misty is now. Verifying an alibi."

"The alibi of a killer, maybe," Mason said, his expression turning dark.

"I don't want you guys to panic," Christy said. "But they left their phones behind."

"What are you talking about?" I demanded while trying to process her words.

"Misty and Zig both left their phones locked in a desk drawer in their dorm room. I know because I decided to track her phone, and it pinged to a locked desk drawer in her dorm room."

"You went to her dorm room."

"I'm sleeping in her dorm room. She's not using it, why would I pay for a motel?"

"You can stay with us," I said.

"In your love nest? No thanks. *I'm* not a third wheel." That with a pointed look at Jeremy.

Mason missed the whole exchange. He was shaking his head. "She left her fucking phone behind."

Mason never said fucking. *I* said fucking. If I were a mermaid, "Fuck" would be the catchphrase under my glamour shot.

"We need to get a look at the employee files," Christy said. "Get an address on Eva Quaid and head there next."

"Why there?" I asked.

"Because the husband still lives there," Christy said. "And what better suspect than the spouse?"

"Employee files it is," I said. "Lead the way."

Christy gave a nod, not even slightly surprised that I'd agreed to trespass. But then she glanced at Jeremy and gave a little shrug. "Maybe you cop types should step outside? Wait in the cars. Plausible deniability or whatever."

Jeremy sucked in a breath, then exhaled, "*That's* the reason."

"What?" I asked. But Mason was nodding as if he already knew.

"She broke up with Jeremy to keep him out of it if she gets into trouble."

I blinked. "It's plausible. It also suggests she's doing something illegal." Then I said, "Must run in the family. Come to think of it, so do cops."

Mason took a deep breath. "I'm going outside to... check on the car. And I require your assistance on that, Jere." Because you know, they were cops, out of their jurisdiction, without a warrant, and Christy and I were about to go snooping.

We stepped out of the private dining room and into the main dining room. The guys headed across toward the front doors. Christy led me down a hall that led left from the big room.

"That's the office, there," Christy said, pointing at a closed door that I immediately approached. "But it's probably lock—"

I turned the knob. The door swung open. We stepped inside. A green four-drawer filing cabinet stood there just asking to be rifled. I opened the third drawer in search of the Qs.

"What the hell is this?" said a gruff and angry male voice from right behind us.

I spun around and slammed the file drawer shut in a single, guilty-looking move. Christy was saying, "Um... We were... uh—"

I took a long step toward him and pointed my finger at his round, unshaven face. He had the beginnings of bulldog jowls just starting to droop. "You're in big trouble, mister. *If* you're trying to take advantage of your employees, that is." I had no idea where I was going, I was just going.

"Who the fuck are you?"

"I'm a lawyer and I want to see this young woman's contract."

Christy rolled her eyes and sent her boss a pleading look. "She's my aunt. I'm sorry Mr. Mackey," she said in her softer, slightly higher pitched Misty-voice. "She wanted to see my contract, and I thought it was the easiest way to uh..." She gave a delicate shrug.

"Shut her up?" he filled in. Then he shouldered past us, reached for a different drawer. He pulled the file out almost without looking and handed it to me. "Have at it, Auntie Lawyer. And as for you," he said to Christy, "This is the second time I've caught you in my office when I wasn't. Once more, you're fired. If the owners weren't coming tonight, I'd fire you right now. Shit."

"The owners? The owners are the VIPs who are coming tonight?" Christy asked. "I thought that was in two weeks."

"Well, it's tonight. They wanted to catch the performers off guard, see how you look when you haven't had any prior warning they'd be there."

"What a bunch of assholes," she said in a voice entirely un-Misty like.

"Hey!" The boss barked, so I stepped between them. "This is actually an amazing contract." Because it was.

"Best in the biz," the manager said proudly. "They own their own images, characters, names. They have to consent to anything we use in publicity. And they're paid by the show, but they also get a cut of the take on any night they perform, and a big bonus when the VIPs come in."

"I apologize for jumping to conclusions."

"I don't write the contracts." He snatched the folder, shoved it into the drawer, and slammed it closed. Then he went to stand in his doorway, sideways, and waved one arm outward to tell us to leave. I glimpsed something on my way by—a photo in the shadows under his desk, of a man gazing at Eva Quaid. Wait, was the man a younger Mackey? The glimpse was brief, as I passed, and I was seeing it from a narrow angle.

But it felt right.

Mason was standing on the other side of the door when we came out, and I was relieved to know he'd had my back. He always had my back. Jeremy was right beside him.

"Excuse me," Mason said to Mr. Mackey. "We're just here to pick up the girls. Girls?" He extended a hand.

We let the guys hustle us through the place and out the front doors since they were the closest. Mason walked a couple of steps behind us, keeping himself between us and mean Mr. Mackey.

"I didn't get her address," I said when we were clear. We still had to walk around behind the building to get to our vehicles.

Mason quickened his steps, coming up between us. "I got a little bit. She worked here for seven years, and her maiden name was Mendosa.

"How the hell do you know that?" We'd circled around to the parking lot in back.

"We didn't really go outside," Jeremy said. "We went back into that private room while you were in the office."

Mason picked up from there. "I took the photo off the wall and flipped it over. You'd be surprised how often you find information that way. It was printed on the back. Eva Mendosa with the date she started and the date of her final performance."

We were getting into our cars. Myrtle didn't so much as pause in her chewy bone chewing. Christy said, "I can't be much help today. First show's at 1:30."

My spidey sense was tingling, and I didn't know why. "I think I should stay. Keep an eye on you."

"Mackey's not gonna let you lurk around before we open. You didn't exactly make friends at your first meeting. Besides, you're meeting my mom at noon to try on a dress."

"Tomorrow," I said.

"It got moved up." She turned her phone toward me.

> Sandra: Why isn't your aunt answering texts?

I grinned, then frowned. "How does she know you're here?"

"What? I'm visiting."

I lowered my head. "We're gonna have to tell her what's going on."

"Nothing's going on. Misty's taken up crime-solving and wanted a weekend to herself to do some shady sleuthing shit. I'm taking her place as a mermaid for the weekend. That's it."

"Except that she left her phone behind," I said.

"And except that she left me, too," Jeremy said.

I scowled at him. "It's just a break."

"I'm worried I left that photo of Eva hanging crooked as hell," Mason said. "When I heard Mackey come in—"

Christy said, "No worries, Uncle Mace. I'll slip in and straighten it."

"Be careful," he replied. And she nodded. "I'm going to head over to the local PD, then."

"Tell me you're not going to report my sister missing, Uncle Mason."

"No. For the record, I think you're right. She's out playing detective."

I saw the pride in Mason's eyes when he said the word detective. That was the look he'd had at Jeremy's graduation from the police academy. He was glowing with pride. "Um, she's out playing *amateur* detective. She gets *that* from me."

"I'll claim half credit," he fired back with a wink. "Jere, you're with me. I bet we can get a look at the files on Eva Quaid. Professional courtesy and all."

"That's brilliant, Uncle Mace," Jeremy said. And that look in Mason's eyes got brighter. He was as proud of his nephews and my nieces, soon-to-be his by marriage, as if they were our own offspring.

RACHEL

"I am so excited for this!" Sandra said when, a short time later, we were sitting in a small but elegant bridal boutique awaiting the dresses I'd liked from the catalogue. Our twenty-something bridal consultant was loading them into a dressing room for me. Before us sat a circular dais with mirrors around half of it and a foot-high pedestal in the center, like the spoke of a wheel.

I was not thinking about wedding dresses.

I was worried about my nieces dying. And trying to figure out a gentle way to break it to my sister that nobody knew where Misty was.

"So about Misty," I began.

"Christy says she's fine. So she's probably fine. I feel bad for sending you out here to spy on her. Maybe we should just go home, after this."

"Maybe," I said. "And I think she *is* okay, but—"

The helper appeared and said, "Ready for you, Rachel." She opened and held the dressing room door.

"Go on," Sandra said. "Find the dress you're gonna marry your guy in. We'll discuss my wayward daughters after."

I sighed in relief, gave her a here goes nothing look, and went to do my duty. I was not buying a dress today. It wasn't the right time. There were mermaids and nightmares in my head and Misty was still out of reach, the little shit. I was going to kick her ass when she got back. Did she not realize how worried her family would be?

No, because her family wasn't supposed to know she was gone, Inner Bitch said.

She never thought that. She was raised in our family, how would she think that? We all know everything.

Not everything.

She didn't need to remind me about that.

I went into the dressing room and turned to close the door, only the helper was in the way. She was a four-foot-eleven redhead who smiled too much, and who apparently thought she was going to help me change my clothes.

"I'll call you if I need you, 'kay?"

"Oh. Okay!" She backed out and I looked past her at my sister, who was shaking her head and grinning as I closed the door. Because she didn't know I'd dreamed of her daughters lying dead in the surf.

A chill shivered up my spine.

Finally, I pivoted to face the dressing room. Five gowns surrounded me like a circle of white lace witches and I actually gasped. There were two on each side and one facing me. It was an ambush!

Something in me whispered, *it shouldn't take an ambush to get me to pick a dress to wear while I marry my soulmate.* I think it was my heart. So I closed my eyes and reminded myself this was important, that I should be fully present for it. This wasn't something I was likely to do again.

Step one, Inner Bitch said. *Try on a dress.*

I stripped off my jeans and T and picked the dress that had stopped me cold in the catalogue. I didn't need help putting it on. Its Grecian neckline draped from my shoulders; its long skirt clung to my hips, its side slit played peek-a-boo with my thigh. I actually exhaled all my breath as I held up my hair and turned this way and that in the mirror. My heartbeat sped up.

Wow, Inner Bitch said. *I didn't think you had it in you.*

I opened the dressing room door, stepped out and up onto the dais, and caught my sister's reflection just as she saw me. She pressed her fingertips to her lips.

"Up on the little stool in the middle, hon," said the consultant, gathering my skirt up like I was too dumb not to step on it. I got up on the pedestal, and she let the skirt go, then fussed with it a little.

"Oh, it has a little train!" Sandra said it like she was saying, "Oh it's made of golden threads mined by trolls and spun by fairies."

It did have a train, but a delicate and subtle one.

Around me, the redhead fussed, pinching here and pulling there. "It doesn't even need alterations. It's like it was made for you."

"That's because it was. I'll take it." I hiked up the skirt and scuffed over to my purse, got out my plastic, and handed it to the girl on my way back to the dressing room.

Behind me, Sandra said, "The first one you tried on, Rachel? Seriously? The first freaking dress you tried on?"

"Do you want me to try them all on and then buy this one?" I called back without breaking my shuffling stride. "Because that's what will happen. This is the one. I knew it when I saw it, and so did you."

I went into the dressing room and peeled the gown off over my head, then took my time straightening it out and positioning it on its hanger.

"Rache, I'm sorry." Sandra's voice came from right outside the door. "I love the dress."

"*I* love the dress," I said, still pissed. "That's what counts, since I'm the one wearing it."

"I'm just... worried, okay? It's weird how little interest you're showing in the wedding."

Because I don't fucking want to mess up what we have!

The thought burst through me so suddenly and with so much force that I clapped my hand over my mouth to keep myself from blurting it aloud. I did not want to mess up what Mason and I had. What we had was damn near perfect.

Well, what the hell do we want then? Inner Bitch asked.

"Well," I whispered, "I definitely want to marry Mason." I took the gown from the hook on the wall. "And I definitely want to do it wearing this dress."

That was going to have to be enough for the moment.

CHAPTER 8

MASON

The Saratoga Springs Police Department was in a brick building that had to be a century old. Its entry door had fancy brickwork arching over the top. The windows were painted with old-fashioned lettering. Nice. There was a small-town yankee feel about the place. Kind of New England, but not quite.

Mason waited for Jeremy in the car, talking to Myrtle the whole time. They'd stopped for an extensive walk in one of the town parks, and she'd seemed to really enjoy it. She'd stopped to sniff a hundred times, did her business, the usual stuff. Jeremy played with her in the fallen leaves. It took all of twenty minutes to wear her out.

"You gonna be all right out here for a minute, Myrt?" He cracked two windows and had parked in the shade.

She settled deeper into her seat. It took multiple rounds of shuffling and snuffling, but eventually she found a position she liked and curled up like a shrimp with her head resting on her paws. She started to snore before her eyes even closed all the way.

"Good then." Mason tucked the white paper plate on which he had written, "*Do not disturb! Anxiety-prone senior bulldog. Interior is cool, temp is monitored, car alarm is loud, owner is cop,*" underneath the windshield wiper blade.

Jeremy pulled into the parking spot behind him. His Firebird was better than ever. He'd been upgrading it a piece at a time. It still wore its original paint job, and the firebird spread on the hood was old and faded. He was saving up to have it restored to its original, with maybe a few custom touches.

He'd inherited Mason's motor-head, for sure. And his career. His kid was a rookie cop, with his first job at the Broome County Sheriff's Department. Josh— Josh was turning out different. He didn't yet know for sure just how.

He got out of the car and met Jere on the sidewalk. "We haven't even had a chance to talk," Mason said. "How are you? You good?"

"I'm not going to drink, if that's what you mean. Nothing could make me take a drink until I know Misty's safe. I might need a meeting later, but right now, I'm focused on her, not me. Not my wounded little heart."

"You're a good man, Jere, but I really was just asking how you're doing."

He looked up, grinned a little. "Sorry. I'm a raw nerve."

"I know. I get it. I'm proud of you, you know that?"

"I do know that. I'm your phone background."

"Yeah," Mason said. His chest was full.

Jeremy's smile faded and his eyes turned serious as he met Mason's. He had to look down, not much, but a little. "What did Aunt Rachel see?"

"Eva Quaid," he said. "I guess she wants to be found."

Jeremy's eyes shifted past Mason's right shoulder. Mason turned to see a woman coming their way. She was tall, for a woman, had dark hair with a few silver strands in the bangs across her forehead, big nose, ready smile, and a badge on her trouser-belt. She extended her hand, and said, "Detective Brown?"

"Detective Scott," he said, gripping for a shake. Her hand was damn near as big as his. "This is Officer Brown."

Jeremy shook.

"Your son?" she asked,

"Nephew," Jeremy answered for him, with a smile Mason's way.

"Nice. It's Jen, by the way. Café Cop is on the corner. Shall we?"

They fell into step in an uneven line that allowed for collapse in case of oncoming pedestrians, Detective Jen Scott leading the way to an outdoor table at The Corner Café. Mason guessed Café Cop must be its *uno*fficial name.

"Hey, Jen," said a young waiter. "The usual?"

"Strong and black as always, Kelly."

"Ditto," Mason said.

"I'll take an iced tea," Jeremy put in.

Kelly was off in a flash.

"So, you said on the phone you're interested in a cold case? The mermaid, right?"

"How'd you guess?" Mason asked.

She rolled her eyes. "You're not the first to ask. You're not the hundred-and-first to ask. But you *are* the first cops, so I figured that was worthy of a meeting. You said you were from, uh—"

"Binghamton."

"And you heard about the cold case on that freaking podcast, and decided, what? To come out here and solve it?"

"Nothing like that," Mason said. "It's personal. My niece works at The Sapphire Club. I don't know, it's just my cop sense twitching. I want to make sure she's safe."

"Ohhhh. Right. Is your niece Misty, by chance?"

"You know her?"

"I met her at the club. Her roommate is the podcaster, you know. Yeah, you know that. So, are you, like, here to get info for the show?"

"Absolutely not. I'm asking a personal favor as a professional courtesy. You have my word as a cop, it won't go further, and nothing I get from you will end up on that podcast."

She looked at him for a long moment. She had large eyes, very round, dark brown. "Exactly what is the personal favor you're asking?"

"I'd like to see everything you have on Eva Quaid."

She pressed her lips together, placed a palm on the table and said, "Okay."

"Okay?"

"Yeah. I have to give it to that Ziglar person anyway. We've had her FOIA request for a— well, you know how it is. It's all digitized. I can send you the files." She tapped her phone, then passed it to him.

He entered his number into her contacts and handed it back. "Thanks very much. I appreciate the help."

"Sure. I'll send the files as soon as I get back to the station."

Kelly brought two steaming mugs and a dewy glass, asked if they needed anything else, and left. They stopped talking. Jeremy added a sugar packet and stirred his iced tea. Jen sipped her coffee and closed her eyes. "Mmm. Perfect."

That inspired Mason to taste his own. It was so good he knew he was going to bring Rachel back. Nobody appreciated a great cup of coffee quite the way his future bride did.

"Was that it? That's all you wanted to talk to me about?" Detective Scott was fitting a lid onto her to-go cup.

"Other than..." Mason lowered his voice. "You were the detective in charge of the case. Who did you like for the crime?"

"Shit, we didn't *have* a crime. No body, at least." She took a deep breath. "This is the one that gets to me. I knew Eva, you know?"

"I didn't know that, no."

"Yeah." She sipped coffee, set the mug back down. "I'm the one who introduced her to Paul." A woman walked by on the street with a dustmop dog on a leash, and while the little dog took eight steps to every one of the woman's, they were still in sync, somehow. "We were in high school together. Not really friends then, but later we were the only two locals at Skidmore, so we hung out." She shook her head slowly, her eyes fixed on the cup. "I should've got him by now."

"Him," Mason repeated, not like a question.

She shrugged one shoulder. "The husband," she said.

"Alibi that's hard to beat, though. He was at an art expo, on camera. He uh, makes metal art. Birds with flapping wings, that kind of thing."

"Got you."

She shrugged and got to her feet. "I don't know. I wouldn't mind a fresh set of eyes on this thing, though. Especially now that it's all been stirred up again." She took another big sip. "And with that, I'm out. This was supposed to be my weekend off. I'm going to the beach." She gave a deep nod. "Gentlemen." And then she left.

JEN SCOTT

Jen Scott carried her cooler in one hand, her portable beach chair in the other, and her towel around her neck as she waded out into the surf, around the tip of the boulder, and then back in again on the other side. This was her secret beach within a horseshoe of rocks, only a hundred and fifty feet from the road.

She wondered if anyone else knew it was there. They must, right? She'd never *seen* anyone else there, though. Eva had known about it. She was the one who'd told Jen about it. It seemed a good place to be, right then. With the anniversary. Ten years. God.

Life was good. Lonely, but good. Her two girls were grown, and not too far away for weekend visits. Her ex was on the west coast trying to become a movie star— his version of a midlife crisis. And she was here, doing her job and watching the waves roll in from a little boulder cove.

It was like a hiding place from the world. Within the boulders, the stress of being a cop in a tourist town where every decision must be weighed against its economic impact, and where every citizen had been recently reminded of the case she'd never solved.

None of this was how she'd have preferred it, but Saratoga Springs was where she wanted to be. She loved it there. She'd never leave.

There were no houses near this spot. The road curved very close, but the boulders blocked its noise.

She sloshed inland once she got past the boulder, then set up her chair while her eyes adjusted, and wrinkled her nose. A fish must've washed up. She unfolded the little beach chair and set it in the sand that was still mostly busted-up seashells if you walked much farther in, and she didn't generally do that, barefoot.

She sat in the chair. It had a little back support, which she appreciated. She didn't remember having backaches every night in her thirties.

Damn, that smell was worse.

She took her towel from around her neck and dried her feet and legs. Today, her feet felt cold. She'd have to start bringing socks.

She looked toward the left side of the half circle of rocks now that her eyes had adjusted to the dimness and saw in the surf a fish tail the size of a dolphin's and... blue.

She started walking toward it, a chill uncoiling from the base of her spine. Shells stabbed her cold feet. Her gaze followed the tail up onto the shore as its blue grew lighter by degrees until it became a human torso, with human breasts, and shoulders, and neck, and a face she knew, even though its skin was mottled and purplish. Other than that, though, she looked perfect. Dead, but perfect. Some of her long, dark curls, entangled with dead fish and crustaceans, had even started to dry.

Jenn whispered. "Eva."

CHRISTY

No thirty-three-year-old-male should ever be a billionaire. That was the conclusion Christy reached, once she closed her jaw and realized who the three assholes who'd just walked into the locker room had to be. The owners. The bad boys.

She'd blurted "Who the fu—" before her brain kicked in to answer her own question.

"You uh, might wanna knock next time, shout a warning or some shit. We change in here."

"We *own* in here," said the leader of the pack.

Christy put her hands on her hips, cocked her head, and opened her mouth. Echo stepped directly in front of her. "We didn't expect you guys until dinner," she said. Coach Hannah came in, and then everyone was trying to get a word in with the guys who signed the checks.

Christy could not have cared less. They were out of their

fucking minds, walking into a locker room like they owned the place just because they owned the place.

The mouthy one was a toothpaste ad, on a beach with a surfboard under one arm, and a flash and sparkle effect when he smiled. Today he wore loose fitting, gray exercise pants made of something shiny. She guessed one never knew when one might suddenly break into a workout. His hoodie said YALE on the front. Because what was the point of having gone there fifteen years ago, if everyone you meet for the rest of your life didn't know?

He was flanked by two Gap-For-Men models, one of whom actually had a sweater over his shoulder and held it there with one hooked finger and the same kind of eyebrows you had right before you threw up.

She listened to the conversation to learn their names. Vomit-face had the darkest hair, the darkest skin, and the darkest eyes.

He was hot.

The other guy had naturally black hair but had bleached it, like he was going to try out for the next boy band. These men did not seem like they were pushing forty. Oh, their skin was puffy and bore fine lines, and their bellies were softly rounded. But the vibe they gave off, the attitude they struck, made it seem as if they'd matured up to twenty-three and hit a wall.

"Misty doesn't seem glad to see us," said the blonde.

"Her family came to town, Mr. White," Toby said. "Surprise visit."

Christy had seen the owners' names in block type on a shipping invoice left lying on the bar by a delivery guy and snapped a photo, so she wouldn't forget them. But she hadn't known which was which until she heard them addressed by name. The beach boy was Barron White.

Toby caught her eye and he held it on purpose, long enough to let her know he'd said the name on purpose to help her out.

Right. Misty must already know these guys.

She tried to wipe off her bitch-face and pretended interest in the conversation. It wasn't hard because the topic had shifted from inane kissing up, to the Missing Mermaid podcast.

"Is it having a negative effect on any of you?" That was Boy Band, Andrew Chay, which meant the hottie was Raphael James. The three of them had bought the place with graduation gifts from their wealthy fathers. Barron White had been quoted in the press as saying, "We always wanted our very own mermaids."

She felt her lip curl as she recalled that bit from the podcast. Her sister's podcast, she thought with a surge of pride. It made her stomach turn to think these three were going to be gawking at her from a private room tonight. Revulsion rose. She contained it.

"Nobody's bothered us over that podcast," Echo said. "At least not me." She looked around at the others.

Jasmine said, "Me, neither."

"And me, no more than usual," Toby added. "Though my mom is all scared I'm not safe."

Echo and Jasmine said, "Me, too," and "Same."

"Is it hurting business?" Christy asked.

"Bumping it up," Barron White said, followed by, "I really love your hair, Misty."

Shit. Her long blonde wig was still lying on the bench. She didn't like the way he was looking at her, either. "I hate yours," she said. "Even Bieber doesn't wear it like that anymore."

His brows went up, and the other two guys laughed out loud. "Told you, bruh," said Andy Boybandy.

She managed not to roll her eyes.

"We just wanted to check in, though." Barron was grinning as if he was in on the joke, rather than the butt of it. "Make sure you were all okay. And let you know we're looking forward to the show tonight."

Did his eyes dip when he said that? Like to her boob area? Her hands clenched as the trio turned to leave the locker room.

"Down, girl," Toby whispered with a shoulder squeeze. "Remember, *bonus*."

The other two laughed, and Christy said, "How much is this bonus that you put up with their shit?"

"I got a grand from each of them last year," Toby volunteered.

Echo and Jasmine found other focuses for their eyes, and Christy knew immediately that they were getting more. Significantly more.

Apparently, the billionaire bad boys were more into mermaids than mermen.

She changed and hoped to God the assholes weren't going to camp out in their private viewing room and watch them practice.

"That's pretty," Toby said, nodding at her chest. She knew he meant the big metal mermaid suspended from a chain there.

"That's a Crisis Companion," she told him. "A gift from my mother. Has a rape whistle, seatbelt cutter, and I don't even know what all. I'm pretty sure in a pinch it'll even dole out good advice."

He laughed and his eyes sparkled. She liked Toby, she decided. She liked them all. They were a good team. Then he got more serious. "Do you know where Misty is? I mean, you don't have to tell me," he added so fast it was all one word. "I just... it's weird she'd try to fool us."

"As far as I know, she's fine." She wasn't going to say anything beyond that.

"Good. That's good." He leaned in closer. "I think Barron White has a thing for your sister. She's been able to dance around it, but he seems a little more intense this visit."

"Well, if he gets out of line while *I'm* Misty, he'll get to meet my ball-kicking shoes." Toby grinned, but Christy didn't. She said, "Do you think he has? Been out of line with my sister?"

"He skirts the line... with all the girls," he said. "But I don't think he's crossed it. Yet."

When Aunt Rachel heard about this, there was going to be a problem. Christy almost smiled just thinking about it.

RACHEL

"I got the files on Eva Quaid," Mason
met back at our home away from ho
back with him, but he was outside, w
the place so she could take in all the sn
could stay with us for the duration, ... we hadn't said
otherwise. It would be hard to feel very romantic with so
much going on, anyway.

Mason and I were in the living room, and he was tapping
his phone. "I just forwarded everything to your laptop for the
bigger screen," he said.

It was mid-afternoon. Christy's early performance was
already done, and she'd texted to say it had gone much
better. The guys and I had agreed to meet here, regroup,
make a plan and head right back out again.

I reached for my computer and handed it to Mason, then
said, "I got something today, too."

"Oh?" he asked, opening the laptop. Then he looked up
over it at me, his attention caught. "*Oh*? The dress?"

I nodded. "Yep. The same one I saw in the catalogue, the
very one I came out here for. As soon as I put it on, it was
like..." I sighed, gave my head a shake. "I can't believe I'm
this sappy about a dress. But it's *the one*. That's all. Sandra
said I'd know when it was the one, and she was right. I told
her she was full of shit, but she was right."

He set the laptop aside. I saw the smile he tried to
contain as he rolled easily off the sofa and wrapped me in his
arms. "I can't wait to see you in it."

"I can't wait for you to see me in it," I told him. "My sister pissed. I think she had her heart set on spending

He frowned at me, and I sighed. "We had a nice lunch together to make up for it. She's decided she shouldn't be snooping into her adult daughters' lives, and she's taking Christy's word that all is well with Misty. So I..." I lowered my eyes.

"You didn't tell her."

"I didn't tell her. I let her go home without knowing that Misty is missing or that she dumped Jere—"

"It's just a break."

"Or that she's a professional mermaid, or that Christy's taking her place in the tank. She thinks she was overreacting and doesn't want piss off the girls more than she already has."

He nodded slowly. "She'd be terrified if you'd told her. And we still have no reason to think Misty won't be back tomorrow, as promised. No reason to think she's in any kind of danger at all."

"Except for my dream thing," I reminded him. But I sank onto the sofa, opened the laptop to pick up where he'd left off, read a few lines, and said, "And now this."

"Now what?" He sat beside me and read over my shoulder.

"Three more people who were questioned in Eva Quaid's disappearance," I said.

"Barron White, Raphael Jones, Andrew Chay," he read, "Owners of The Sapphire Club."

"They were there the day Eva vanished," I said, skimming

the reports in search of their alibis, their statements, anything.

"Who was there the day Eva vanished?" Jeremy and Myrtle had come in through the front door just as I'd spoken. Myrt lifted her head, sensing my location and heading toward me with as much confidence as if she knew the place by heart, though she couldn't possibly have learned it already. She reached me and butted her head hard into my shins. "Ow," I said, then bent to boost her up onto the sofa beside me. She turned around twice, then laid down and settled her head onto my thigh.

"The bad boy billionaires," I said. "That's what the merfolk call 'em."

"The owners? They were suspects?"

I turned the laptop screen his way and he took it with him to a nearby overstuffed chair, sat down, and began scrolling.

"They were questioned and cleared," I summarized for him, "but I haven't found their statements yet, so I don't know details of their alibis."

"Rich guys can *buy* alibis," Jeremy replied, and there was a hint of alarm in his voice. "And these three particular rich guys were at the club a few minutes ago."

"*What*?" Mason and I blurted in unison.

"Christy texted while I was walking with Myrt— who has a new spring in her step, have you noticed?— to say the owners were there, two weeks ahead of schedule. They'd left the club for now but will be back to watch the last show of the night."

"Like a surprise inspection?" I asked.

Jeremy picked up his phone and read Christy's text aloud. "'I hope to God one of them is guilty because,' green vomit emoji."

"We'd better get the hell back over there," I said. "Christy said to wait until later, but I don't like this."

Jeremy nodded. "I want to hang back, check on some of the other suspects listed in Detective Scott's files. Especially the husband."

"But Jere, Christy could be in danger."

"So could Misty," he said. "And going to check out the original suspects is the only thing I can think of that she and her podcaster pal might be up to."

"We need to cover both girls at the same time," Mason said, his eyes on mine. I saw what was in them; the knowledge that I'd dreamed about both girls, not just one.

"There are several other suspects who were on Detective Whatshername's radar," I said.

"Jen Scott," Jeremy filled in.

"You guys better tag team them. I want Misty found and I don't want to wait for tomorrow. I can't keep this from my sister that long. It wouldn't be right. And if anything happens, and I haven't told her— she'd never forgive me."

"You're right," Mason said. "If we don't locate Misty tonight, we probably need to talk to Sandra and Jim."

I squeezed his hand, acknowledging our two-people-one-mind connection. "So, I'll keep an eye on Christy and the bad boys at the club. You guys go track Misty down. Which of you is taking Myrt?"

CHAPTER 9

CHRISTY

Mr. Mackey was in his office. Muffled tones with pauses in between came through the closed door. He was on the phone with someone. Christy soft-stepped almost all the way to his door, then ducked into the private dining room across from it, closing the door behind her. Then she stood still while her eyes adjusted. The place was dim, but the pool that formed one entire end, cast rippling blue waves onto the other three walls. The curtains in the outside windows were all drawn. Had they been drawn before?

She scanned the photos on the walls, spotted the one of Eva, hanging at such a sharp angle it would not have gone unnoticed. She went to straighten it.

"For the life of me, Misty—"

She stiffened at the female voice, then consciously

relaxed her spine as Coach Hannah went on. "—I can't figure out why you're always in here looking at these old photos."

She was about to say this was her first time in the room when she realized the coach meant *Misty* had been in here looking at the photos.

"I just can't help it," she said, softening her voice. "They're all so beautiful."

"*We*, darlin'. *We* are all so beautiful." She walked to the photo just two frames to Christy's left and straightened it, though it was already straight. The photo in the frame, Christy realized as she studied it anew, was a younger Hannah, rocking a blue and white tail and matching seashell bra.

She averted her face to hide her sudden suspicions. She had questions. Her gaze fell on her twin sister's photo on the opposite wall, among the newest. Her pose was sheer grace, and Christy knew how hard that was to pull off. But there was Misty, like a crescent moon. The gentle arc of her back continued down through her tail, and all the way up through her long blonde hair, flowing in a perfect continuance of the arc. Her eyes were open and facing the glass. But she wasn't smiling. She wore a sad, yearning expression, her brows bent with some unknowable ache.

God, she was beautiful.

"I love your hair, by the way," Hannah said. "But not for performances."

Christy pulled her backpack around to show the blonde wig sticking out the top. "Of course not."

"How's that muscle strain? You gonna be all right today?"

"The back's better." Unless she screwed up again.

"Mostly. And I was thrown off by my family showing up unexpectedly." It was a really good lie, she thought.

"Well, don't let it happen again," Coach said, then she gazed at Misty's photo. "Give me *that* mermaid, today," she said.

"You've got it." As they walked out of the room together, she said, "Did you know her well? The mermaid in the photo I was admiring?"

"Eva? We swam together three seasons before she disappeared." Then she frowned. "But I told you all this already."

"Right, you did. I know. I just... can't stop thinking about her."

"Well, today's not the day for that." But she walked back to Eva's photo, pressed a fingertip to her lips, and then to Eva's smile. "Today is important. You need to be at your very best."

Christy nodded and turned to hurry up the stairs to the pool area, pulling on the wig as she went. The gang were all there, including a handful she hadn't met before, who might not know who she was yet. She hoped. They were all talking and laughing. Nobody looked at her in any odd way.

"Okay, okay." Coach Hannah clapped her hands. "We're running the routine, tails-off the first time through. Change up and hit the pool."

Misty's tail was in the locker room where Christy had left it earlier. The thing was heavy, so she was happy to leave it there a little longer. She stripped down to the black tank suit, standing in front of her open locker, and taking her time so she could be the last to leave. Maybe they'd all be in the water, already warming up, and too distracted for conversations. Because she had to pretend she knew these people. And that was not an easy thing to fake.

MISTY

"I promised my sister I'd be back by tomorrow," Misty said again. "If I don't make it, or at least check in, she'll call out the National Guard. Just so you know."

It was late-afternoon. They'd watched Paul Quaid's cabin all day, and the son of a gun still hadn't left.

"He's going. Any time now, he's going," Zig said. "Look how many of those metal-animals he's carried out of the workshop."

She was looking. It was hard not to. The pieces were lined up like soldiers in front of the small outbuilding, every single one unique. There was a duck holding an umbrella, a fairy sitting on a mushroom, a peacock in full display, and an eagle with wings that moved when the wind blew. Paul Quaid was really good at what he did.

The sound of a vehicle came, and its rumble was so much like Jeremy's precious Firebird, it made her heart hurt. And then that very car rolled into the gravel driveway and shut off. Misty gripped Zig's forearm so hard her nails dug in.

"It's Jeremy," she whispered. "Dammit, what is he doing here?"

Zig sent her a wide-eyed look, then they both backed up into the shadows cast by the pine trees all around them.

Jeremy got out of his car and Paul Quaid came out of the workshop welding helmet tipped up, pulling off his over-sized gloves.

They spoke. Misty couldn't hear what they were saying, but Jeremy showed his badge to the guy and then asked him some questions. Paul Quaid answered no to all of them, if the direction of his head shakes were to be trusted.

Jeremy nodded and headed back to his car, but before he got in, he stood in the space of its open door and looked around with keen, intent eyes. Misty sidestepped behind a tree trunk, and prayed the camo of their tent fly would fool him.

"He's looking for me," Misty whispered.

"Guess your dumping him didn't take."

Jeremy's gaze swept right between them and he frowned harder but kept going, finished his perusal, and finally got into the car.

"Maybe I should go find a phone so I can call him and ask why he's looking for me." Then she looked back down at Paul Quaid, who'd returned to the workshop, then came out carrying two more sculptures. One was a cartoon bulldog that made her smile. That had to be a good sign, right? "I think you're right, Zig. I think he's going to leave soon." She couldn't abandon this, not when they were so close. Not even to call Jeremy.

But she would call him later. As soon as they finished their mission here, she would call him. God, seeing him had made her heart crack and fall into a thousand pieces. She ached for him. She almost wished he'd seen her there.

She closed her eyes.

"You really love that guy, don't you?"

"I really do," Misty said. "But I love what we're doing, too."

Zig shrugged. "Don't just assume you have to choose between them, though. Okay? I think there's a way you can have both."

"Really? How?"

"Didn't say I knew how, just that there's a way. There's always a way."

"Sounds like something my mom would say. Or Aunt Rache."

"My mom's been saying it my whole life," Zig said. "And I've seen it proven true more times than I can count."

Misty tipped her head to one side. "Actually, so have I."

RACHEL

I sat at a table in the shadowed recesses of the dining floor where I could see everything I wanted to see and not be too noticeable myself. I watched every patron who came and went throughout the waning afternoon. The curtains were closed over the tank, but I knew the merfolk were in there, rehearsing for their next show. Mason still hadn't come back, and he hadn't texted an update in more than an hour.

It made me antsy.

There was commotion over by the entrance. Three drop dead gorgeous forty or so males had come in. They were wearing the entire wait staff's income in brand names, and they were loud. To me, people who are loud in public places are shouting, "Hey! Notice me! I'm important!" And also, frequently, "I have more money than you!"

Mr. Mackey came hurrying from that little hallway to the right of the tank, smiling so widely I had to do a double take to be sure he wasn't just some happy dude who *looked like* Mackey. But no, it was the grouchy asshole himself, grinning and pumping hands, first with the loudest one of all, he of the extra-long blond side-bang and clothes he probably thought were cool. The others deferred to him, and Mackey practically bowed.

I'd done my research. I knew their names and faces. They'd bought the place ten years ago, and Earl Mackey had been a mere bartender. Barron White was the leader. Raphael Jones and Andy Chay were his business partners and sidekicks. There were handshakes and shoulder claps all around, and then the entire group crossed the length of the room, talking as if everyone really should be able to hear them. They were staying at "the cottage up at Shoreline." They'd arrived this morning and decided to "pop in early and see what really goes on around here." Har har har.

Barron White veered behind the bar and helped himself to a couple of bottles from the top shelf, then rejoined the others at the far end.

He caught me watching him, though, and winked at me so I flipped him off. He burst out laughing, rejoined his cohorts and they chortled and all the way into that private room with a full wall of glass through which they could ogle the mermaids.

My phone chimed. Mason. It was about freaking time. I answered with, "A bad boy billionaire just winked at me. You should watch me better."

"You want me to punch him in the nose?"

"I'll let you know. What's up on your end?"

"Kind of a lot. I need you."

"Where?"

"Eventually, the morgue."

"What?" My blood drained all the way to my feet. "Mason, what the hell is going on? I can't leave Christy here, not with the boy band full of suspects who just showed up."

"There's a band?"

I rolled my eyes. "We need backup."

"Look toward the entrance."

I did, and there was Mason standing with Jeremy. They made their way to my hidden table, which I guess hadn't been so hidden. Then again, they were both cops, and they both knew me pretty well.

I hugged Mason's neck. He kissed mine. I clasped Jeremy's shoulder. "You didn't find Misty, I take it."

He shook his head, lowered his eyes. "Not yet."

Mason said, "We hadn't finished looking. Jeremy was going back out tonight, but we got a text from Detective Scott. Eva Quaid's body was found."

I felt my eyes widen and looked at the guys in turn. And then I frowned. "Now? After ten years?"

"I know," Jeremy said. "And on the weekend of her disappearance, just when the mermaid podcast has everyone in town talking about her again." He looked at Mason, then me again. "It has to be connected. All of it."

"Jen Scott says that Eva looks like she died yesterday. And uh— she was wearing her tail. There'll be an autopsy early tomorrow morning. She's trying to push the ME to do it overnight instead. But she says we can come in now if we want."

"Oh," I said.

"Jeremy can stay here to watch out for Christy. We'll resume looking for Misty right after we see the body. Okay?"

"But there are three perfectly good suspects in that private room in the back."

"Don't worry," Jeremy said. "I'll keep an eye on things."

CHRISTY

Christy managed to execute the corkscrew move directly in front of the tank's right side, beyond which blurry forms watched from the private dining room. She had decided to do it for Misty after Toby had given her a stern lecture. Maybe she was offended by those assholes, he'd said. Who wasn't? But their bonus checks were real money that Misty was counting on. He said she never would have left if she'd known the owners were coming tonight and that Christy could make or break her sister's budding *career*.

So she'd decided that, if she wanted to take a stand against the patriarchy, she should not do it while pretending to be her sister. She would just be mild-mannered and shake her tail at them so Misty could collect a big fat check.

She couldn't see the trio very well from inside the tank, especially when in constant motion. She was supposed to be gathering softball sized fake pearls from strategically placed fake oyster shells. Which meant they had a view of her ass inside the tail, or her boobs behind the clam shells. It irked her.

This wasn't their only mermaid club, Jasmine had told her when she'd probed for a little background info. A performer who caught their eye might get to move up to one of their bigger venues in New York or L.A.

So she did the damn descending spiral, and gathered pearls, and as she swam away, she glanced over her shoulder and added a sassy tail flip. Then she froze, squinting because she was pretty sure Barron White had his fucking hand in his fucking pants while he watched her.

Enraged, she flipped him off and swam to the surface. She loved the power her tail fin gave her. It propelled her upward like a missile. And then she smashed her head into a solid ceiling that shouldn't have been there. Her yelp was swallowed up in its own bubble of air, as she held her head and sank, but then someone had her by the arm and was pulling her up and out of the water, and he was shouting, "Who the hell closed this? Here, here—" It was Raphael Jones. He must've raced up the stairs when she'd crashed into the cover. He was kneeling over her on the floor beside the pool.

"Get off her," Jeremy said.

Jeremy was here?

She opened her eyes, still holding both hands to the top of her head, and looked between her bent elbows at two faces. One was Jeremy's and he looked pissed and worried. The other was the dark, handsome, older guy with a pair of expensive sunglasses on his bald, brown head. Behind them Coach Hannah and the other performers were crowding in.

"I think I'm okay." She sat up. Jones tried to help. Jeremy glared, and he backed off with his hands up, letting Jere do the honors. The pool cover was only partly closed, she noticed. "I'm pretty sure that was wide open when I went in."

"We'll check the security footage," said Jones. "I'll get to the bottom of this."

"You one of the owners?" Jeremy asked.

"Yeah," he replied in a kind of shitty tone, but then pressed his lips tight as if to check himself and extended a hand. "Raphael Jones."

"Jeremy Brown."

"I'd offer to help you stand, Misty, but, um—" Jones looked down at her tail with a grin.

She saw the way Jeremy was looking at him. He didn't like the guy. He wasn't jealous, obviously. He was head over heels for the good twin. But he was family, and in this family, they protected each other. God knew there'd been plenty of need for it.

"You guys can go," she said. "I'll be fine."

"I'm going to insist you get checked out by a doctor," Jones said. "Technically, I'm your boss, so I can do that. The club will pay for everything, and I'm afraid I can't let you perform again until you get medical clearance. All right?"

Oh, thank God. No more fucking mermaiding. "Yes. All

right, I mean, I hate to do that. Obviously. But if you insist, then I guess I have no choice."

He grinned at her and got up to his feet. Coach Hannah was dressing down everyone in the room, demanding to know who'd closed the pool with a mermaid in the water. That was a huge no-no. She finished shouting and came to her side. "Are you all right, Misty?"

"I think so."

"I'm taking her to the local ER," Jeremy said.

"Saratoga Hospital is closest," Coach replied. "You know where it is, Misty."

Yep, I bet Misty does know where it is, Christy thought. Then she flopped onto her belly, and called out, "Zipper!"

"I got it, I got it." Echo came behind her and attached a long pull to Christy's hidden zipper. Leaning back and low, she pulled it down. Christy wriggled out then sat there in her spandex and rubbed the circulation back into her legs.

Jere reached down and she let him pull her to her feet. "Aunt Rachel thinks the owners make damn good suspects," he murmured, leaning close enough so only she could hear. "Keep your guard up with that guy."

She didn't mention that she'd heard "that guy" might have a thing for Misty. No point throwing fuel on that fire.

Jeremy walked right into the locker room with her. No one else was in there, anyway. The other mermaids were already starting their part of the show. She could hear Mackey on the loudspeaker, reassuring the audience that the injured mermaid was fine, and that was the moment she realized her collision had been witnessed by everyone in the entire place.

She changed her clothes fast while Jeremy prowled the locker room, checking out its customizations as curiously as she had her first time in there. A row of lockers had been replaced by a long counter backed in lighted makeup mirrors, with stools affixed to the floor in front.

Heading to the sink, she ran cold water on a paper towel and pressed it to the gaping place welling with blood on top of her head. "Dammit, this might need stitches. Where's Aunt Rachel? I thought she was staying."

"Let's talk about it on the way," Jeremy said, but he said it softly. Then he crushed a little cold pack he'd found somewhere and handed it to her.

They headed down the back stairs to his car while she held the cold pack and a wad of paper towels to the top of her head. Jere used his phone to set a route for the hospital.

"I hope there's a walk-in. I'm not going to an ER for a little bump on the head." She got into the car.

Jere got in the driver's side, looked at her, and immediately reached past her to yank fast-food napkins out of his glove compartment. "You're bleeding right through those," he said.

She took the extra napkins in one hand and twisted his mirror her way with the other. There was blood kind of pulsing from under the ice pack. She lifted it and shoved a fresh wad of napkins there, pressing hard.

"Maybe the ER," she said.

He drove above the speed limit, and she felt dizzy. To keep from passing out, she asked, "So where's Aunt Rache?"

"Same place we're going, actually."

A chill raced right up her spine and her eyes shot wider. "Aunt Rachel is in the hospital?"

"Not like that. She's in the uh... the morgue. They found Eva Quaid."

Christy's jaw dropped. "Damn. Misty picked a bad day to be out of touch."

CHAPTER 10

RACHEL

Mason spirited Jen Scott and their hospital staffer-guide away on some paperwork bullshit he'd made up on the spot to give me a few minutes alone with Eva Quaid.

I stood beside her, staring at her. That wasn't my best method, but it was where I began. There was another table to her right with her mermaid tail laid out on it. She'd been wearing it when she'd been found, washed up on the shore of Saratoga Lake. It was every shade of blue from powder to midnight, and as bright as it had been in the photo.

Her skin was stained in splotches of fuchsia, purple, and slate-blue-gray. She hadn't been in the water long. She wasn't puffy or bloated. She hadn't decomposed a day, not in ten years. There'd been a smell, Jen Scott had told them, but it was from the flotsam tangled in her hair. She was perfect. And aside from the purple bruising, she looked as she had in the photo. In fact— I leaned closer— she was still wearing makeup.

Waterproof makeup. Inner Bitch had a knack for pointing out the obvious.

Her long, dark curls had dried since she'd been lying there. There were bits of seaweed in its tangles, along with minnows, crayfish, twigs, leaves. Her eyes were closed, her face relaxed, her mouth slightly open. There hadn't been an autopsy yet, just the preliminary exam.

You gonna do the thing or what?

I ignored my inner voice and kept looking with my eyes. Her hands were purple, her knuckles looked like she'd been in a fistfight with a boulder.

Time is wasting. They'll be back soon.

I dragged my gaze from Eva to the table beside her, where her silicone tail laid, zipper down, looking as lifeless without a mermaid inside as Eva's body looked without Eva inside.

Then I closed my eyes and put my hand on her forearm. I flashed back to the tank, the ride-along, so it felt as if I was the mermaid, pounding on the glass while my lungs tried to tear through my chest. I yanked my hand free and sucked in a breath so deep it hurt.

"Shit, you didn't touch her, did you?"

I turned to see that Mason had come back, but the pliable orderly was no longer with him. Instead, a black woman with close-cropped white hair and a matching lab coat was looking from me to the corpse in alarm. I didn't know where Detective Scott was.

"Of course not," I said. "I know better than that, I consult with our PD back home."

"Binghamton," the woman said, having been told by Mason, I presumed.

I nodded and offered a hand. "Rachel de Luca."

"Mm." She didn't offer her name in return, but her badge did. Dr. Kay Sharpe, followed by 40% of the alphabet. She wasn't looking at me, but scanning the room, the body, the tail. "You've seen what you needed to see?" She hadn't come all the way in but was still standing near the door as if ready to hold it open for us to get the fuck out.

Instead of replying, I continued moving up the side of Eva's table. I needed another moment to close my eyes and feel.

"Is it just me, or is her head misshapen?"

"Blunt force."

"Is that what killed her?"

"I don't think so. There's no skull fracture. But I've only had her here for seven hours. Autopsy is scheduled for tomorrow morning, but the Detective in charge—"

"Jen Scott," I filled in, to show her I knew. "Mason had coffee with her earlier. We're consulting on this, informally."

"Yes, Detective Scott. She asked if I could do it tonight, so I'm here." Her attitude had eased a little bit. "Do you want to observe?"

No, no, no, no, no.

"I wouldn't know what I was observing," I admitted. I knew a lot of things, but a doctor, I was not. Still, I wanted to get a little more. I felt in my belly that Eva had more say to me.

"Well, then, I need to get underway." Dr. Sharpe opened the door.

"Sure. I just need to um…"

Pray! Inner bitch shouted.

I blinked. That wasn't bad. "I'd like a moment to honor her spirit before I go."

Frowning, Dr. Sharpe slid a questioning glance at Mason. "She native or something?"

"Just… deeply spiritual."

"*Deeply,*" I agreed.

She crooked one eyebrow like she knew I was full of shit. But it wouldn't be PC to voice her skepticism about my religion aloud. Thank goodness for the woke mind virus. I lowered my head and closed my eyes.

It slammed into me like a tsunami, the same as before. Eva, as Mermaid Esmeralda, was banging on the front of her tank. But I saw more this time, because I was seeing her from the *out*side, this time. There was a dark trickle of blood following her hairline, from the center, down the left side, down past her ear in a red-black strand. A droplet pulled free and floated upward along with the bubbles of her last breath, all the way to the black, closed ceiling atop the pool.

And then I saw the life leave Eva Quaid's eyes.

My phone pinged, my eyes snapped open, I sucked in a breath, because I hadn't in far too long. Mason's hand closed on my shoulder. It felt like he was flowing steadiness down my spine to my liquid knees.

I glanced at my phone.

Jeremy: Christy is OK. Minor injury. In ER.

"Something happened to Christy!"

"He says she's okay." Mason had received the same text. He was looking at his phone.

"People who are okay do not go to emergency rooms."

"You'd be surprised," Dr. Sharpe began, but then she bit her lip, nodded once and pointed through the open door and down the hall. "ER's that way. Follow the signs. I hope everything's okay."

I sped out the door and heard her call after me. "When you see her, tell Detective Scott to get this tail thing out of my morgue."

RACHEL

Christy was sitting on a stretcher with her legs over the side, holding an ice pack on top of her head when Mason and I got to her. Jeremy and a woman were in with her, far more people than were allowed. Mason said, "Detective Scott. I wondered where you went."

"Yeah I saw Jeremy with your niece and got distracted." She nodded a hello to me, and I nodded back, but went straight to Christy, and hugged her hard, then pushed the cold pack away so I could see beneath it. There was a dark trickle following her hairline from center down the left side past her ear in a red-black strand. Exactly like the one on Eva's head. Exactly like I'd seen in the vision.

I went icy inside. I saw a little droplet float upward from Christy's head toward the ceiling. But it wasn't real.

"It was the stupidest thing." Christy's voice pulled me back. "Apparently the cover was never opened all the way, and nobody noticed. I swam up fast near the side, smashed my head."

I blinked and looked at her. "The pool cover? The Jimmy-Stewart-Wonderful-Life fucking pool cover? I'm going to kill somebody," I said in the presence of three cops.

"It was an accident, Aunt Rache. Kind of my own fault. I got pissed off—"

"Pissed off at what?"

"I'm pretty sure one of the gawking owners was tugging his pug while he watched me perform."

Everything in me went cold.

Mason said, "Oh, shit."

I cracked my neck and said, "Mason and Jere, take care of Christy. I forgot something at the club."

"Rache—" Mason began.

"I did, too," Jen Scott said. "Forget shit at the club."

"You weren't at the club," I said.

"Sure I was. Just not today. I'll drive."

RACHEL

Jen drove her ancient Ford Bronco with the windows down, possibly to cool my rage. The wind was good, cool, and tasted like spring. The red haze cleared from my vision and we drove awhile in silence.

"Nice car," I said at length. "Mason's into the classics."

"Me, too," Jen replied. "Even my everyday ride's an old Crown Vic. Trunk the size of a small garage."

"Nice."

We fell silent for a few miles. Eventually, she said, "So what did you make of Eva's body?"

"We barely had time to look at her before we heard about Chri—Misty."

"You called her Christy in the hospital, too."

I averted my eyes. She was a good cop. "Mind's the first thing to go."

"I looked Misty up, you know."

"No, I don't know. On what grounds?"

"Routine background on her podcasting roommate. It's obvious she's working with her. So I know she has a twin. I'm pretty sure that's Christy in that hospital room and that she's covering for Misty in her mermaid duties."

"What makes you think that?"

"Because I spoke to Misty at the club a couple of days ago. But when I approached her in the hospital, she'd clearly never seen me before."

"Head injury," I muttered.

"Oh, come on. Where the heck is Misty?"

I met her eyes, so she wouldn't think I was lying once I thought up a lie.

"Oh, wait. That's what you're here trying to find out, isn't it? Is your other niece *missing*?"

I had been trying to read her ever since we'd got into the

car together. Even leaned my head back against the seat and closed my eyes. But there was nothing. It was like that with Mason, too. Maybe it was a cop thing. Except I had no problem picking up emotions and stray thoughts from Mason's partner Rosie, or Chief V. Maybe it was only a *certain* cop thing.

I sighed away my resistance. "She took off for the weekend and didn't tell us why. Her mother is worried. So yeah, we came to verify she's okay. Just to ease my sister's mind."

"And have you?"

My brain warred between telling her so we could get some official eyes looking for Misty, and keeping my mouth shut so my niece wouldn't hate my guts when she got back.

"She's fine. Boyfriend problems." I made a face. "Nothing dangerous, though."

"Thank god. I was worried for a minute." She turned off the highway.

"Us, too."

"So when we get to the club," Detective Scott said, then stopped and started over. "I want to kick ass and take names as bad as you do. But I also want the truth. And I just..." She shook her head rapidly, like a dog trying to shake a flea. "I missed something. I need to start this whole case over. Go back to the beginning." She took another turn. We'd be at the club in five minutes.

"How the hell does Eva look the same age?" I asked. "How has her body not decomposed?"

"I don't know," she said. She glanced sideways at me. I

decided I liked her. "I'm hoping Sharpie can tell us that, tonight."

"Sharpie. Cute."

"She's good. Albany's her home base. I put in a request for her as soon as I found the body."

"Wait, wait, wait. *You* found the body?"

She sent me an eyebrows-up nod. "Listen, this is not for public consumption," she said. "There's this little cove on the eastern bank. You can't get to it unless you walk out into the surf, around its boulders. It's my favorite spot. When I got there this afternoon, she was there in the surf."

I swore under my breath, then whispered, "What are the odds?"

"That was my first thought too. That it was deliberate. Somebody put her there on purpose, because it was *my* case. And that was *my* spot. But I've been studying the currents today, remembering past visits, too. The lake brings a lot of flotsam in there. I usually leave with a few souvenirs in my bag. Six-pack rings, fast food cups. Found a pair of Ray-Bans once."

I could imagine the spot and felt sad about garbage washing up on its shore. "I want to see that cove."

She frowned at me. "County forensics team went over it with a fine-tooth comb."

"Oh, sure they did," I said. "I didn't mean for business. It just sounds... special." And maybe I'd be able to feel something there.

"Oh." The word pitched up, as if in happy acknowledgement of a connection made. "So what did you guys think? About the body?"

I thought a lot of things. I thought the cause of death would be drowning, and that the water in her lungs would be chlorinated. Pool water, not lake water. I thought her knuckles were destroyed from pounding on the glass walls that stood between her and her next breath. But of course, I couldn't say any of that. So I offered up a provable observation.

"She had a head injury that looked just like Christy's."

Jen turned my way fast, and I drew the line the blood had made, from my part, down along my hairline and in front of my ear.

She put her eyes back on the road and used the Lord's name in vain.

"I don't want Christy back in that tank," I said. "But she's of age, and the doc at the ER gave her medical clearance."

"I don't want her back in that tank, either," the detective said. "I don't want *any of them* back in that tank."

I nodded hard. "Listen, I didn't want Mason with me because I might do something illegal, and I don't want to fuck up his work life. I don't want to fuck up yours, either."

She looked at me and wiggled her eyebrows. "How illegal?"

Goddammit, I did. I liked her. Didn't I have enough cops in my life?

RACHEL

Jen Scott and I stood in the pool room, looking down into the tank. The cover was fully open. Two of the mermaids were performing. From above, their antics in the water appeared as if through a carnival mirror, distorted and warped.

"Detective Scott, good to see you again."

We turned away from the pool to see the three who'd been in that private room earlier. *Filthy fucking pigs* was probably written all over my face.

Jen said, "Rachel de Luca, this is Raphael Jones, one of the owners."

He held out a hand.

I looked at it in disgust. "Are you the one who was fondling your junk while my niece performed?"

His face went as lax as if he'd momentarily lost brain function. The two assholes behind him laughed.

"You think it's *funny*?" I took a step closer to the pair, learning in, "You think it's fucking *funny*?" They backed up as one. You'd have thought it was choreographed. "Who shut that fucking cover while she was in the pool?"

Raphael held up his hands, glancing between us as if he thought Jen would jump in any second. But she seemed content to let me growl.

"We don't know. Our club manager suspects it was never opened all the way."

Jen said, "Jeremy— the mermaid's friend who took her to the ER— said you were going to check the surveillance."

"We did," Jones said. "It um, wasn't on."

"It wasn't on?" I asked.

Jones shook his head. I noted the beach boy who'd been doing all the talking when they'd first arrived, had nothing to say.

"Our manager says it was an oversight. He didn't even know it was turned off."

"I'm gonna need to see that equipment and the recordings," Detective Scott said.

"As soon as you get a warrant." Ah, at last word from the blond Barron.

I took another step closer, leaning in. "You're exploiting young women for profit in unsafe working conditions with sexual harassment on the side. You want to fuck with me? You want to fuck with my kid, *Chad*?"

"It's Barron," he said, but he stuttered on the B.

"Full name, address, and current contact info," Jen said as I backed off. "On all of you. And that—" She pointed at the wall-mounted box that controlled the pool floor. "Needs to be disabled until further notice."

"Disabled?" Barron White asked.

"Yeah," she said, "As in, unbolt it from the wall, disconnect the wires, and hand it over."

"Or option B, I take a sledgehammer to it," I added, moving toward the box as I spoke.

"Whoa, whoa, wait a minute, now. What's going on here? Is this some kind of investigation?" Raphael Jones asked. "Misty bumped her head. It was an accident."

"It was an accident?" I said. "Someone *accidentally* turned off the surveillance cams and then *accidentally* closed the cover while she was in the pool?"

"While there's a dead mermaid on a slab in my morgue with a nearly identical head injury?" Jen Scott added.

The three men went dead silent. They stopped moving. They looked at each other, and then at her. "They found Eva?" That was the one who hadn't spoken yet, with the shock white hair and too much gel; Andrew Chay.

"Yeah," she said. "So, it's a little more than a bump on the head we're investigating. And I'm gonna need you three to stay in town until further notice."

Two rolled their eyes, the third, Raphael, asked, "How is Misty?"

I wished I knew. "She's fine." Then I nodded at the box on the wall. "You gonna call your maintenance guy or should I go find a hammer?"

CHAPTER 11

MISTY

The ten-year-anniversary of Eva Quaid's disappearance was tomorrow, if you counted by Sundays. And if Misty and Zig found what they needed tonight, maybe her case could finally be solved.

Paul Quaid hadn't left his cabin yet. But he had driven his beat-up car around behind the workshop, and when he'd returned to the driveway, he had a trailer hooked to the back. It was an enclosed box trailer with doors in the rear.

It was pitch dark when he finally started loading his sculptures into the trailer.

"This is it," Zig said. "He's loading up."

"It's about freaking time." Misty rearranged herself on the ground. They were sitting behind the fallen log with their folded sleeping bags as cushions. It felt like the darkest night ever in the forest. The moon hadn't yet risen. It wasn't silent, though. Night birds called, sounding hoarse and lonely.

Insects chirped and whirred, and small animals skittered through the underbrush. The breeze was light and chilly and it smelled of pine.

She couldn't bring herself to leave, not even to find a phone in the nearest village, so she could check in with Jeremy or Christy. Not when it looked like the guy was finally going to leave. She wanted to get a closer look at that corkboard wall, and maybe at the computer on the desk, too.

So she stayed, and she watched.

Paul Quaid carried one sculpture at a time out of the shed. Each was wrapped in a padded blanket like furniture movers use. He handled them as if they were made of crystal. He put about ten pieces in the trailer, which would hold ten times that many, she thought, then he stood behind the thing for a moment.

He was a thin man, slightly stooped, but that was bad posture, not old age. Or maybe he was bent by grief. Or evil. He was thirty-nine, according to their research. Dirty-blond hair, kind of shaggy on his head. He brushed his hands together, gave a nod, and walked toward the dark cabin.

"No," Misty whispered.

"Shit," Zig said as Quaid went inside and closed the door. "Is this guy ever leaving?"

Misty watched the cabin's inside lights come on. They had the layout down, from their previous window peeping. The kitchen light came on. About a minute later, the bathroom. "Not the bedroom, not the bedroom," she prayed.

"Not yet, anyway," Zig whispered. "Kitchen light's still on. He never leaves a light on behind him. Maybe he needed a potty and snack break."

"What do you, teach preschool?"

"Nephews." She grinned and Misty understood the playful spark in her eyes. They were close and they both knew it.

"Bathroom light's off," Zig said. A second later the kitchen light went out as well. They watched, holding their breath, staring so hard at the little cabin that it should've rattled the windows.

And then a light came on in the little room with the paper- and photo-filled corkboard wall, and they saw him walk past the window that faced them, coffee mug in one hand.

"Coffee break," Misty said on a relieved sigh. "He's gonna work on his murder wall, while he enjoys a cuppa Joe."

"If he does this after every ten pieces, we'll be here all night again." Zig looked her way. "You want to go back to town, find a phone and call... anyone?"

"Christy. I'm going to call Christy. And no. We're too close."

She looked down at Paul Quaid. He stood before his corkboard and sipped his brew so slowly, Misty wondered if he knew they were out there and was torturing them.

But eventually, he walked back the way he'd come, and the light went out. A moment later, he was outside again. He'd left the mug behind.

They settled in to continue watching him as he loaded his precious cargo at the pace of a sedated sloth. And predictably, they both nodded off.

The slamming of the trailer doors startled Misty awake. She had no idea what time it was. Zig had brought all the camping gear. Misty had no travel clock or plain old, analog watch. Her sole contribution to their survival was her dumb-ass Crisis Companion. If they needed pepper spray, a tire pressure gauge, or to escape a submerged vehicle, it might even be helpful.

Zig straightened up beside her. She'd been resting her cheek on the log, and its bark pattern had stayed behind.

"This is it," Misty said. "Look, look."

"I'm looking, I'm looking."

Quaid closed and locked the workshop. Then he went to the cabin and went inside.

"He's just locking up the house, unplugging the toaster or whatever," Misty said. "My dad used to do that before every family trip."

"You took family trips?" Zig sounded as if she hadn't.

Before Misty could say anything, Quaid came back out of the cabin with a black satchel. He turned to lock the door, then went to the car, slung the satchel in ahead of him, and got behind the wheel.

"Hallelujah!" Zig said. And as the car rolled down the driveway with its trailer rolling behind, she got up.

"Wait," Misty said, grabbing her wrist. "He's barely even out of sight yet."

"He's gone. He's heading to the art show. He won't be back anytime soon."

"Unless he forgot something," Misty said.

Zig sighed, then said, "You're right. We'll give it an hour, let him get well on his way, all right?"

Misty nodded, then got up and stretched. They'd been so still for so long, she was stiff and achy. Zig got up too. She went into the tent and came back with a pair of granola bars.

"Thanks," Misty said, taking hers and unwrapping it. "I can't believe we're this close."

"I'm glad you're as into this as I am," Zig said.

"How can I not be? I work where she worked. I see her picture on the wall there. I don't know, something about her speaks to me." She took a breath, sighed hard. "It's more than that, though. This is the most fun I've ever had." She bit off half her granola bar. "Screw it," she said. "Let's get down there now. I can't stand waiting."

Zig grinned. "Neither can I."

It was scary as hell creeping out of the woods to cross the stream and then the open ground to the cabin. They approached from behind, but even so, the fine hairs on Misty's arms rose and her skin tingled as soon as she'd stepped out of the sheltering trees.

There were twenty yards to the cabin's back door, in knee-deep grass and wildflowers. "We should crouch really low, so the grass conceals us," Misty whispered.

"From who? A passing deer?" Zig waved an arm at the surrounding forest. There was a winding dirt road out front, but there hadn't been any traffic. Other than Eva Quaid's widowed husband, there was nothing out here at all.

So Misty followed Zig as she strode through the meadow, sending up puffs from every plant she pushed past. At first, Misty thought it was pollen, then she realized there were bugs in the puffs, too. They were disturbing the hell out of an entire universe of bugs. There wasn't a sign anyone had ever walked through this meadow, and she felt uneasy. Paul

Quaid obviously wanted solitude. They were invading his privacy, trespassing in his home, and maybe his grief, as well. If it turned out he was innocent, they were doing something very wrong.

Zig was already at the back door, jiggling the knob. "I need something to break the glass."

"Yeah, no," Misty said. "Let's try all the non-destructive options first." She moved to the nearest window and found it unlocked. It slid upward with a little nudging. It was a bathroom window, but full-sized, easy to climb over. Yet, she hesitated.

Then Zig pressed her hands to the windowsill, jumped up, and slung a leg over. A second later she was on the inside looking out. "Come on, hurry up." And then she turned and walked away, and Misty heard, "Holy shit. Get your ass *in* here!"

Misty pulled her sleeves over her hands so she wouldn't leave fingerprints, and climbed in. The bathroom was narrow and blue, and its door stood wide. She hurried through into the small room. There was a desk, a chair, and that entire wall littered in papers and photos, mostly shots of Eva with other people whose heads were either circled or crossed out.

The papers were news clippings, pages from police reports, even a couple of witness statements were pinned to that wall.

"All it needs is red string connecting pushpins." Zig took out her disposable camera and started snapping photos while Misty moved nearer and tried to make sense of the display.

"Some of the people with their faces crossed out are for sure alive," Misty said. Because her first thought had been the opposite; that Paul Quaid was a serial killer, and these were his past and future victims. "All the billionaire bad boys are up here. Two of them are crossed out."

"Mr. Mackey too," Zig said. "And strangers. We should try to ID them later."

She snapped close-ups of the photos of people they didn't know, then put the camera back into her pocket and turned to the desk.

"Hey look. Is that one Detective Scott? There's Coach Hannah, too."

"All the suspects." Zig lowered her camera and met Misty's eyes.

They were both thinking the same thing. Why would a killer be investigating his own crime? And that was sure as hell what it looked like he was doing with all this. Investigating and maybe ruling people out.

Zig turned away, raised the camera again and snapped.

Misty went to the desk. It held a lamp, a desktop computer with an oversized, fat-ass monitor, a laptop, and an open book: *Crime Scene Forensics.* A pool of light painted the murder wall, then moved over their faces as a car pulled right up to the front of the cabin. It stopped. Its engine shut off.

Misty shot Zig a terrified look, then glanced back toward the bathroom and its open window— their escape route, but it was too far. The front door was already swinging open. She grabbed Zig by the arm, and they moved behind the desk and ducked into its ready-made cave.

Misty held one hand over her own mouth, and clutched Zig's upper arm with the other. Zig was listening— Misty could tell by the way her eyes narrowed, the way her head titled. "What is that?" she mouthed with barely a sound.

Misty lowered her head all the way to the floor to peer out from under the desk, then bit her lip to keep from yelping. Someone was being dragged by his arms, through the front door, into the house. It was Paul Quaid. The motion stopped, and his head fell left, so he was facing them: His eyes were open and blank, and Misty bit her knuckle to keep from screaming. A blood trail painted the floor behind him, and she thought it was good she wasn't seeing the back of his head, where it originated.

The person dropped him, then stepped over his unconscious or possibly dead body and back outside.

Misty started to back out from under the desk, but Zig grabbed her arm and shook her head with urgent eyes. Then the door opened and the person came back inside. Black lace up boots, like you'd wear for hiking. Jeans.

There was liquid sloshing, and the sharp smell of gasoline.

Zig swore very softly. Misty's mind was racing, screaming at her to zoom out from the desk to the bathroom and scramble out that window before the killer could strike a match. And then it was too late. There was a whoosh and heat, and liquid fire spilled toward their hiding place.

And then, the eyes staring at her blinked.

RACHEL

We brought Christy back to our increasingly crowded romantic getaway. Myrtle, who'd been shuffled around too much, bounded out of the car without my help, trotted ahead, nose-dived into the grass, rolled onto her back, and wiggled in joy. I turned to assist Christy instead, since Myrt clearly didn't need my help.

Was it weird that it hurt my feelings?

Very weird, said Inner Bitch.

Christy didn't need my help, either. But she had the good sense to accept it anyway. I walked her inside with my arm around her shoulder.

"I don't like that Jeremy's going back up there all alone," she said.

"He's a police officer," I replied, even though I was as uneasy as she was. Jere said he'd had an odd feeling when he'd driven up to Paul Quaid's cabin earlier. He'd been compelled to go back. But Mason had to go to the morgue, where the autopsy on poor Eva Quaid was wrapping up. The ME had promised to wait for him to arrive, and to share her findings when he got there. Jen Scott had backed up my "consulting unofficially" line, and we were in.

"You don't need to stay with me, you know," Christy said. The door creaked when I pushed it open and we stepped into the foyer, then to the stairs. "This place is great."

"Yeah," I said. "I think you'd call it an English garden out back. There's a hot tub with a view."

She frowned, looking at Mason, then at me again. "This really *was* a romantic getaway, wasn't it?"

"Until it became a family emergency," Mason said. Then he met my eyes. "But frankly, kid, our whole lives are a romantic getaway."

I gazed back at him and Christy rolled her eyes. Then Mason's expression turned serious. "We have to call your sister, Rache. You know that, right?"

"Not yet," Christy said. "We need to make sure Jere is okay. That's our priority after finding Misty. Traumatizing my mother is way low on the list."

As soon as she said it, my phone pinged. I glanced down at it, then smiled and turned it toward Christy.

> Jeremy: Checking in. All good so far. Don't let Christy send you after me. She's the one in danger.

I raised my eyebrows and tilted my head, the universal body language for I told you so.

"Whatever." She plodded up the stairs and waved a hand back at me. "I'm fine. I can use any bedroom, right?"

"Yeah, except the one Jere's using. You'll see his stuff." I sighed and turned to go back to where Mason waited with a mug in his hand. I smelled chocolate.

He always knew what I needed and when I needed it. I'd never been able to read him the way I could read everyone else. But over time, it had started to feel like we were renting space in the same brain. I didn't have to read him the way I read others. I just *knew* him.

And he knew me.

He said, "Would you have preferred vodka?"

"Nope. This is perfect. Besides, I locked it up soon after Jere got here."

"I think he's in control. I don't think seeing it around the house would trigger a relapse."

"Having it around the house while knowing he's addicted to it would just feel callous to me," I said.

"I thought so too. Went to move it, but you already had."

"You're too good to be real, you know that?" I cupped his face and leaned up to kiss him.

When our lips parted, he said, "So how'd it go at The Sapphire Club?"

"We made them remove the cover closing mechanism. Took it right off the wall."

"Detective Scott let you do that?"

"She's the one who ordered it. She took the thing with her for safekeeping. I mean, I'd have preferred to take a sledgehammer to it. Her way was less satisfying, but it didn't result in jail time."

"Always a plus," he said. He turned me in his arms, and we walked toward the master suite with our cocoa, and our bulldog shuffling along beside us, following the scent of chocolate. "Surveillance show anything?"

"It was mysteriously turned off," I said. Anger yanked on my neck muscles. I tilted my head left, then right trying to ease them. "Nobody saw anything. The owners are each other's alibis, and I suppose Jeremy would've seen if any of them had left their private room to go upstairs. He said Jones ran up just ahead of him, and the other two were still in the VIP room."

"So that leaves... who?" he asked.

"Anyone could've sneaked up there from the back stairway, and tried to close the cover," I said. "Patrons, wait staff, bartender, the other merpeople, even."

"That's an interesting thought," he said. "How competitive is the mermaid biz? Any love triangles going on among them we should know about?"

"We can ask Misty when we find her. By the way, Jen knows it's Christy in the tank. She offered help find Misty, but I told her she was fine. It was just boyfriend trouble."

"She promised Christy she'd be home tomorrow," Mason said. He opened his mouth to say something more, and then his phone went off in his hand: a video call.

"Dr. Sharpe," he said, holding the phone out in front of him. It was dim in the foyer, so we walked to the kitchen, where he'd left a light on.

"Detective Brown, Mrs. Brown," she said. I didn't correct her. "Detective Scott gave me the okay to call you with the autopsy results rather than making you come all the way over here for them. The cause of death was drowning, not the blow to the head. That came first but wasn't fatal."

I had already known that, of course.

"The water in her lungs was chlorinated," she went on.

I had suspected that as well. So far, nothing she'd told us was news.

"But how did she look as if she just died," I asked, "and not a day older than when she vanished?"

"She'd been frozen."

"Frozen," Mason repeated. "So someone put her body into a freezer, kept her there for ten years, then just now decided to take her out and dump her into the lake? Why?"

"That's above my pay grade," Dr. Sharpe said, even though she made more than him and they both knew it. "But she hadn't been out of the freezer for more than twelve hours. Her core temperature was still colder than the water."

"Tenth anniversary," I said softly. "The podcast, all the renewed interest. Maybe it was all too much for the killer. Maybe they thought once her body was found, it would put the whole thing to rest."

"I'm not a profiler," Dr. Sharpe said. "There's something odd here; a dog tag, you know, military? It was lodged in her throat."

"Whose name is on it?" Mason asked, and I held my breath.

"PFC Paul R. Quaid," she said.

The fucking husband.

Mason said, "Thanks, Dr. Sharpe. I appreciate the info." He disconnected and looked at me.

My heart clenched up in my chest and I whispered, "Jeremy's on his way up there."

MISTY

Misty and Zig sprang to their feet from behind the desk. A wall of fire blazed between them and the front door, roaring ever closer, but there was a straight, flame-free path to the bathroom where they'd entered. Zig grabbed Misty's arm. "Come on!"

"We can't leave him there!" Misty shouted back as fire climbed the walls and licked at the ceiling. The curtains flashed, blazed, and blackened all in seconds, and smoke burned her eyes.

She dropped to her knees, pulled her shirt collar up over her nose and crawled to the man on the floor until she could get hold of his shirt sleeve, and then she sat back and pulled.

His pants leg was on fire. She could barely move him, but then Zig took hold of his other arm, and the body came along with ease. They were each stooping, clinging to an arm and dragging as fast as they could. They made it into the bathroom, cleared the door, and Zig slammed it, while Misty grabbed a towel to smother the flames on his jeans. Under the towel, burnt denim mingled with burnt skin and the smell made her gag. Then Zig yanked the towel off him and crammed it against the crack under the door to buy them a few more minutes. Seconds, maybe.

"Let's get him out the window," Misty said.

"Let's make sure he's not already dead fir—" The dead guy interrupted her with an agonized moan. "Shit," she said. "Okay, let's go. Get him up."

They each grabbed him under an arm and hefted him right up over the windowsill. Smoke was pouring in around the closed bathroom door. There wasn't much time.

"Climb over him, pull from the outside," Misty said.

Zig did, and she wasn't too gentle either, scrambling over the guy who lay half in and half out. She landed on the ground outside, grabbed his arms and pulled. Misty wrapped her arms around his thighs and tried to lift and push, but her lungs and eyes were burning, and she started coughing and lost her grip. When she glanced behind her in panic, the door had warped so much it had swung open, and she could see the flames in the room beyond it. They'd nearly reached the desk, and the laptop that sat there. She fell to her knees, put her head and shoulders between the guy's legs from behind, and lifted for all she was worth. He shot out the window so fast he took Zig to the ground with him, but she sprang up and reached back for Misty.

Misty looked back into the room. The laptop was sitting right there.

Then she threw a big towel into the tub, cranked the taps, and picked it up again to drape it, dripping, over her head. She ran to the desk, grabbed the laptop, and it was so hot it burned her hands and she dropped it to the floor. Smoke blanketed her and drove her to her knees. Zig was screaming for her from outside. She grabbed the edges of her wet towel and used them to pick up the laptop, shoving it along the floor ahead of her as she scramble-crawled to the bathroom. The door was open, and the entire doorframe was blazing. She shoved the computer ahead, then pulled the towel around her face and rose enough to run through. She tried to close the door, but it was sizzling hot, its paint bubbling, and too warped to move.

She was overcome with a fit of coughing and fell to her knees again. She heard her name in a high-pitched shriek from outside. Zig.

And then another one came from inside her own head.

Get the fuck up, Misty! It was Christy's voice. Loud and clear. *Get the fuck up and get out right now.*

She pushed herself up off the floor. The room was full of

smoke, but she felt around and found the computer. It was still hot as hell. She tugged the towel from her head and wrapped it around the laptop, pushing up to her hands and knees. And then she crawled and hoped she was moving in the right direction. Her head hit a wall. She started coughing again, and every cough made her inhale more smoke. Her eyes were watering so hard and burning so much that she couldn't open them at all. She clasped the towel-wrapped computer to her chest, pressed her free hand to the wall and used it to help her pull herself up, feeling for the window ledge. There! There it was. Curling her fingers over the ledge, she pulled herself to her feet and pushed the computer through first.

Then someone was gripping her forearms and pulling her bodily up the wall and out the window. Not Zig. Way stronger than Zig. Somebody male. Big hands, and strong arms that pulled her into them and helped her stumble away from the heat and smoke. Jeremy's arms! It was Jeremy's arms around her, his chest beneath her head. She'd know them anywhere.

"Get—" *Cough, hack, gasp.* "—the laptop."

"Get away from there! You're too close!" That was Zig, shouting back at them from the driveway. Misty managed to open her eyes but could only make out a hazy shape standing near a lump on the ground that she hoped was Paul Quaid.

Jeremy scooped the computer-towel bundle up off the ground, keeping one arm around her as he led her away. When they reached the road where Jere's classic Firebird was parked, he opened the door so she could sit down on the passenger seat. He put the laptop on the floor, then reached past her for a water bottle and handed it to her. He searched her face in the dashboard lights. "Are you hurt?"

"I inhaled a little smoke, but no." She coughed a little more, then focused on inhaling the cool, pine-scented air. "How are you here?"

He shrugged. "You were missing. Everybody's here."

"I'm not missing."

"Because I found you," he said just as Zig crowded in beside him to lean into the car and see for herself that Misty was okay.

Jeremy squeezed her shoulder, then turned and ran back to where Zig had left poor Paul Quaid lying on the ground.

"Guy still had his cell phone in his pocket," Zig said. "I couldn't believe there was enough signal to call 911."

Misty heard distant sirens already. "How the hell is Jeremy here?" she asked, as if maybe Zig would have the answer.

"You mean that hero hottie who pulled your ass out of the fire? That's Jeremy?"

"Yes, that's Jeremy. And I thought you were gay."

"I am bi. *Very* bi at the moment."

"Yeah, well, he's taken."

"By who?"

"By me," she said.

"I thought you said you were on a break."

Misty watched Jeremy tending to Paul Quaid. He had a first aid kit he'd taken from his car trunk, had already cut away the burned pant leg and was pouring cool, sterile water over the burns. He was speaking in that low, easy tone that could calm anybody through any sort of trouble. She loved when he used that voice. She'd called it his good-cop voice, but he'd had it before. Probably picked it up from Mason.

"Misty?" Zig prompted.

Misty blinked. "Yeah. Break's over."

She got out of the car, pushing past her friend, but then she looked back and said, "Quaid's laptop is on the floor. It got pretty hot, but maybe it's not entirely destroyed."

Then she headed to Paul Quaid and knelt across from Jeremy beside him. The guy was moaning and moving his head back and forth very slightly.

"This wasn't an accident, Jere," she said softly, and she ran a soothing hand over the victim's cheek. "Somebody dragged him into the cabin, already unconscious. See his head?"

"I see it."

"They poured gas around and dropped a match."

"You witnessed that?" He met her eyes and she nodded. "From inside?" Again, she nodded. "Did the arsonist see you in there?"

"No. Absolutely not. We were hiding under the desk."

"Where's your car?"

"We parked at the trail head and hiked in. Been camping," she nodded toward their site, "over there."

He studied her face, nodded once, then said, "Do you want to tell me what you were doing inside Quaid's house when he wasn't home?"

"No. And I'd prefer not to have to tell anyone else, either."

The sirens grew louder. Jeremy twisted his lips to one side, which he did when he was wrestling with a problem that needed a quick solution— like he was wringing the answer from within. It was just one more of those little quirks she loved about him.

And then he said, "Okay."

"Okay?"

"Okay. I don't want some crazed arsonist coming after you. Are you sure you're okay?" She nodded. "Then you and your friend get the hell out of here. Take a roundabout route back to your campsite and clear out. Quietly. Do not be seen. Don't leave anything behind to say you were ever there. And then get back to the Springs so Rachel, Mason, and Christy can stop worrying about you."

"Aunt Rache is there?"

"Where else would she be?"

She sighed, lowering her head. "I didn't mean to set off a full family panic, you know."

He softened his tone, reached across to stroke her hair off her forehead. "I'm really glad you're okay."

She covered his hand with hers. "I'm sorry I put you in this position, Jere. It's the whole reason I—" She stopped talking and instead, leaned up and pressed a kiss to his mouth. "Thanks, Jeremy." Then she hopped to her feet and ran back to Zig, reached into the car and grabbed the towel-wrapped computer. "We have to go, Zig. The dude's still unconscious and Jere's got our backs. Come on."

CHAPTER 12

RACHEL

"Jeremy? What's wrong?" I answered on speaker because Mason was driving.

"Nothing's wrong. Misty is okay," Jeremy said. "But you didn't hear it from me, because I never saw her."

"Never saw her where, Jeremy?" I closed my eyes, so I could feel him. I saw fire, and my eyes flew open wide.

"I'm at a crime scene north of you," he said, not knowing we were already on our way to him. "Paul Quaid's house was torched with him inside, unconscious from a blow to the head, I surmise. Apparently, he came around long enough to stagger outside where he collapsed."

"That's a lot of surmising, son." Mason looked like he'd heard the missing parts of the story as clearly as I had.

"He was... lucky," I said.

And Inner Bitch said, *Luck had nothing to do with it.*

Jeremy said, "She's heading back your way, getting us a motel room. It's late. We can have the family reunion tomorrow, she needs some sleep. But she's okay."

"Is Quaid going to be okay?" Mason asked.

"I don't know." Jeremy's voice was low, and I felt his doubt. "He's still unconscious. EMTs just got here. Local cops are right behind them, I gotta go uh... explain my presence." The connection was broken.

"She was there," I said. "Misty was at the scene of what sounds like an attempted murder and arson."

"She was up there investigating Eva Quaid's murder for that podcast." Mason managed to look worried and proud at the same time. "The tenth anniversary edition, I bet."

"Wait a minute, wait a minute," I said. "This weekend isn't just the anniversary of Eva's disappearance, it's also that art show that was Paul Quaid's alibi according to the police report. The one he never misses. He shouldn't have been home."

"Bet about now he wishes he wasn't."

It was after midnight when we spotted Misty's Jeep in the other lane coming toward us. Mason flashed the headlights so she'd know it was us, then made a U-turn and sped up behind her.

She pulled onto the shoulder and got out, came running, and hugged my neck like there was no tomorrow. She smelled like smoke, and the terror she'd experienced rippled through her, into me, so I hugged her harder. "Are you okay, baby?" I whispered into her fire-scented hair. God, was it *singed*?

"How do you even do this all the time?" she asked, and I had no idea what she was talking about.

She let go of my neck and hugged Mason's. He was giving her his stern cop face, though. She let go of him and took a step back, which brought her beside her companion, a girl with tight corn rows, and killer eyes. And then she smiled and flashed her braces.

"Hi, Aunt Rache," she said, trying to look angelic.

"You must be Zig. What the fuck were you doing?"

"Investigating," Misty answered. "Don't judge us. You've been doing it for years."

"Well, yeah, but—" Mason began before I cut him off.

"What were you thinking? You could've—"

"I saved a man's life tonight, Aunt Rache."

Well, that shut you up, didn't it?

Sure did, IB. Sure did.

"Look, everything is fine," Misty said with a softer tone. "We were never there."

I lifted my brows and sent her a look. "Tell me you didn't ask Jere to lie for you."

She said, "I would never *ask* him to." But she lowered her eyes when she said it. "Look, we're exhausted. I just want to get some rest. We can talk about everything else tomorrow."

"Go to the house we rented for the weekend. I'll jot down the address."

"I have it," Mason said, pulling a card from his pocket.

"But I don't want—"

"Look, we can't be everywhere at once," I said. "Christy's there. It's safe or we wouldn't have left her alone. Nobody here

209

knows where we're staying." I took the card from Mason and tucked it into the pocket of her jacket. "Wait. I have your phones. Christy got them from the dorm room. They're both dead, but you can take my charger. Don't plug it in until you're where you should be. We don't want it pinging way the hell up here."

"Okay."

Mason had retrieved her phone and a charger from our glove box, and he handed them to her. "You heading straight to bed?"

"Zig and I need to decompress first."

"You sure you don't need an ER first? You're hoarse, and you reek of smoke. How much did you take in?"

"A little."

She didn't elaborate and the look in her eyes said she wasn't going to. I was less thrilled about her plan to "decompress" with Zig. The two of them were still digging, and probably had some ill-gotten evidence to examine. What I wouldn't have given for ten minutes alone in that car.

"Thanks for my phone. And for racing to the rescue." She hugged my neck, then headed toward the Jeep, and Zig fell right into step behind her.

So did I. "Listen, um, stay away from the club, okay? There was an incident. Christy got hurt and—" Misty spun around, wide-eyed, and I held up both hands. "She's okay."

"What happened?"

"Cover wasn't open all the way. She hit her head," I explained. "Detective Scott was so pissed she took the control box right off the wall so it couldn't happen again, pending investigation into the incident."

"Detective Scott?" she asked.

"Yeah. She's been really helpful."

"Bitch wouldn't help us," Zig muttered.

Mason shrugged. "Cops don't think very highly of crime podcasters."

"Because we solve crimes they couldn't?" Misty asked, feisty as I'd ever seen her.

Maybe she's found her calling, Inner Bitch suggested.

"That wasn't a shot," Mason said. "And the reason is, they tend to rile up the public. That can make our job harder."

"Thanks for the support, Uncle Mace," she snapped.

"You're welcome. I forwarded you the police reports and the autopsy notes."

She softened her tone considerably. "Thanks."

Then she went the rest of the way to the car and got behind the wheel. Zig hurried around the passenger side to get in. Misty leaned out her door and called, "See you at breakfast." She slammed the door and pulled away, heading south.

I sent Mason a palms-up shrug. "What the hell, with that one?"

"Let's get to the crime scene before all the good evidence is gone." He slung his arm around my shoulders, and we walked back to the Solterra.

RACHEL

The sky was turning from deep blue-black to gray where it showed through the trees. The smell of wet, charred wood hung like a soggy blanket in the pre-dawn air, and we stood breathing it, in front of the smoldering Quaid cabin. Its log walls were intact, on the outside, at least. There was a gaping hole in the roof and a few broken windows. From what I could see through those windows, the inside had burned black.

"I can't figure how he managed to get out," Detective Jen Scott said. "Can't ask him. Still hasn't regained consciousness."

I nodded, and wondered what Paul Quaid would have to say when he did wake up. If he did. I was distracted, because I could feel my wayward niece all over this place. Misty had been there. "Have you seen the autopsy report?" I asked Jen.

"I *have* it," she said. "Haven't had a minute to read it. Why? Have *you*?"

Mason and I nodded in unison. I squeezed his hand, passing the baton. He said, "Paul Quaid's dog tag was in the back of her throat."

She went very still, blinked twice, then said, "That's it then. I've *got* him. Finally."

"It was chlorinated water in her lungs," Mason went on.

"She drowned in a pool," Jen whispered. Then, "She drowned in *that* pool. That's it. I'll get a court order to shut the place down. It's a crime scene."

"A ten-year-old crime scene," Mason said. "Is a judge apt to think there's anything there to find?"

She shrugged. "Maybe not. But given your niece's accident, and the similarity of her head injury to Eva's..." She trailed off and shook her head slowly. "We have to make sure it's safe for the mermaids before we let them back in."

There were still too many pieces that didn't fit in my mind, and therefore I could be pretty certain, in Mason's mind as well. If Paul had killed Eva, who'd tried to kill Paul?

And then Mason asked my question aloud, word for word.

"So if Paul killed Eva, who the hell tried to kill Paul?"

"That's a damn good question." She paced away, turned, paced back. "What if someone besides us knew Paul was the killer? What if this was vengeance?"

I could see it.

Mason could too, because he was nodding. "The anniversary, the publicity from the podcast, it might've pushed them over the edge."

"It would have been someone who loved her," I said, and I thought of Earl Mackey, the club manager, who maybe had a photo of him and Eva under his desk.

"That doesn't narrow it down much." The detective turned to face the burnt-out cabin. "Everybody loved her. Even the fucker that killed her." She stood that way for a moment, then sighed and turned our way. "I suppose that's where we start. With everyone who cared for Eva. Account for their whereabouts."

"Including Mackey," I said.

"And the owners," Mason added. "Who probably only lusted, but still."

"I sent my guys to the bad boys' hotel the minute I heard

213

about this," Jen Scott said. "I'd have gone myself, but I was halfway here. The bad boys were snug in their suites, though."

"You were halfway here?" Mason asked.

Yeah, my ears had perked at that part, too.

"To notify Paul about Eva. I didn't have the heart to do it by phone." I bent my eyebrows at her, and she said, "Okay, I wanted to see his reaction."

I nodded. That tracked. "Did someone check on Mackey?" I asked.

"Home alone. No witnesses. But my guy was at his door at three a.m." She made her voice louder. "This fire started when, two?"

"Call came in at 2:07," one of the firefighters said. Maybe the chief. He was a round man with bushy white eyebrows.

"Mackey was in his jammies, looked like he'd been sleeping," Jen Scott said.

Mason rubbed his chin. He did that when he was putting jigsaw puzzles together, too. "There's no way he could've set the fire at two and been back in his bed at three. Ditto the bad boys."

Jen said, "And before you ask, here." She ripped a sheet of paper from a pocket sized notepad like it was 1990, and handed it to me, since I was closest. Three names I already knew; Andrew Chay, Barron White, Raphael Jones. But the sheet included their hotel, room numbers, home addresses, and cellphone numbers.

"Thanks." I might've sounded surprised she was handing me evidence. I wasn't even a cop. I was *with* a cop who had no official business here.

"It's nothing you couldn't get yourselves. I figured this would save you some time," she said. "Assuming you're still looking into this."

Her phone rang and she picked it up, listened, said thanks, and looked at us again. "Quaid's awake. Doctors are determining whether he's up to an interview now. You want in?"

"You bet your ass we do," Mason said. Then he glanced at Jeremy, who'd been unusually quiet. "Go on ahead," he told her. "We'll be along shortly."

"Sure." Jen headed out, but we hung back to talk to Jeremy, who looked rough. Soot on his arms, blood on his clothes, his hair was a mess.

"I'll come with you to the hospital," Jeremy said. "They'll let me clean up in the ER."

"They will?" I asked.

Mason nodded. "Cops and ER staff have an unspoken agreement," Mason said. "We have each other's backs."

"And then I'm catching up with Misty," Jeremy said.

"Listen, Jeremy, I don't know what happened here," Mason began. "But... be careful with your badge, okay? It's important. Sacred, maybe."

"Uncle Mason, I—"

"Let me finish. Protect your badge. Unless there's something more important in need of protecting. I trust you to know when that is, and what it is. And I will always have your back."

Relief dragged a smile across Jeremy's face, and he hugged Mason hard. "Thanks, Uncle Mace."

"I'm proud of you," Mason said, clapping him on the back.

It was probably just the smoke in the air making my throat tighten and eyes water.

RACHEL

When Mason and I walked into the hospital, we didn't have to ask where Quaid was. Two cops were standing outside door of his room. Jen was one of them. The other was a sixty-plus, whipcord lean man with a face like shoe-leather, snow-white hair, and a mustache that would make a dust mop jealous. He wore a uniform and a badge, Saratoga County Sheriff.

Jen said, "Sheriff Rasmussen, these are the people I was telling you about, Detective Brown, Rachel de Luca."

"Folks. Appreciate your intent, but uh—"

Mason held up his hands. "Hey, we're only here to help. We don't want to get in the way of your case." Then he shook the man's hand. "Good to meet you, Sheriff."

"This is way too many people!" A nurse, a redhead I could feel was all business and super good at her job, came waving her hands like she was shooing pigeons off a park bench. "There's a waiting room right through those doors. Sheriff, you have a call. You can take it at the nurse's desk."

The sheriff nodded, then pointed a finger at Jen. "Nobody in or out 'til I come back."

"On it," she said, then she moved to stand beside the hospital room door with her back toward the 227 on the wall.

I looked at Jen and shrugged. She said, "I'll get you in fast as I can. Promise."

"Thanks."

The nurse leading Sheriff Rasmussen away sent us a glare over her shoulder, so Mason and I retreated into the waiting room. Jeremy was just coming in. He'd hung back, because Misty had called, and the expression on his face was lighter and more cheery than was appropriate for the situation. Worry cleared from my mind like dark clouds driven by a warm wind. Then a little bit of darkness returned. I hoped she hadn't used her own phone.

"What's the update?" Jeremy asked.

"Detective Scott and Sheriff Rasmussen get to go first," Mason said. "I'm not sure we'll get a shot at all."

"Which is fine, because that way I get take my turn with you. Your uncle's pep talk back at the scene was great. But now you get to hear mine."

"Ah, hell."

"You're a rookie cop and you're—" I stopped, looked around the waiting room. No one was around. I lowered my voice all the same. "You're risking your career. Your future."

"Like Uncle Mace hasn't done the same for you? For me? for Josh?" He walked to a chair but didn't sit in it. He stared down at it instead. "It was *Misty*. And she wasn't doing anything wrong. Really. A little wrong, but..." He heaved a sigh and turned to face us as a bunch of racket broke out behind the double doors.

I got up and pushed them open to see people in scrubs

racing into Paul Quaid's hospital room, past Jen and the sheriff who were standing outside the room trying to see past the crush of bodies.

"What happened? What's going on?" I moved toward them and kind of herded them away from the door. They were blocking the flow of staff.

"I don't know. I think— I think he's dead." Jen pushed a hand through her hair and rose on tiptoe to try to see him. The door was still open, so we could see the backs of the people who surrounded him. Yellow scrubs, blue scrubs, scrubs covered in cartoon cats.

Sheriff Rasmussen gave Jen Scott's shoulder a brief squeeze, a fatherly sort of gesture. "Don't know what happened," he said. "We went in to talk to him, and he was... gone." He shook his head. "I know dead when I see it, and he was gone."

I looked at Mason and bunched up my eyebrows. He acknowledged my feeling without even changing expression. Something wasn't right here. I looked around, thinking maybe the dead guy would put in an appearance. I even closed my eyes, not giving a shit how odd it might look.

Hey Paul Quaid, I thought at him. *You can talk to me if you need to. I can usually hear.*

But there was nothing. Mason put his hand on my shoulder, and I opened my eyes to see Jen and the sheriff looking at me oddly. Jen said, "I know it's a lot. Maybe I shouldn't have brought you guys in."

A nurse came out, the same one, but she looked frazzled and sad. "I'm so sorry. He's passed."

"How?" Mason asked.

"Looks like he stopped breathing."

"Due to...?"

The sheriff and Jenn had turned to look at the nurse, which meant looking straight at Paul Quaid, who was standing in front of her. He was translucent, and dressed in filmy echoes of his clothes, all burnt, torn, and sooty. His face was sooty, too.

"He just inhaled too much smoke," the nurse said, and Paul's head moved left, then right, then left, then right, leaving a ripple of itself behind with every motion.

I clasped Mason's hand and felt his attention shift my way.

"Sometimes, the heat damages the lungs, and they just can't recover," the nurse went on. "I'm so sorry."

Paul shook his head again, and then he raised a hand and touched the back of his head.

"Were there any... other injuries?" I asked. I was shifting focus between the nurse and the apparition. I did not often see them this way. I usually *became* them, saw things from their perspective, like doing a ride-along inside their head.

As soon as I thought it, I was looking out through someone else's eyes as they— we— left a diner with a paper-wrapped mushroom and kale breakfast sandwich. It smelled delicious. My stomach growled. Not my stomach, the stomach of the person whose memory I'd entered. He was thinking that he didn't get take-out often. This was a ritual, though. Once a year, the weekend of the big art show, he had this sandwich.

We headed to the car, unwrapping the sandwich on the way.

Then there was a blinding explosion of white light. The sensation of crushing pressure on my head came a half-second later, and with it the most intense pain I'd experienced. I felt as if my head was imploding.

Because it was.

When I looked out through my own eyes again, Mason had moved me bodily. We were in padded, vinyl waiting-room chairs and his was pulled out at an angle that blocked me from seeing the others. Oh, right, and them from seeing me.

"I said we needed a private moment."

"Was it obvious?" I could still see Paul Quaid. He'd followed us in there.

Mason shrugged. "It was obvious to me. You okay?"

"Somebody bashed him in the head from behind. He didn't see their face. It happened at a diner less than an hour from here." I rubbed the back of my head. "He never got to eat his goddamn sandwich."

"Anything from his hospital bed?"

"Nothing." I looked across the waiting room at him. He was hanging out by the door. "He's in his street clothes, not a hospital gown. I don't think he knows what happened in there, or at least, that's not what he's wanting to tell me. Oh. He's gone." He'd faded like a rainbow when the sun moves away, leaving a kind of blush where he'd been, and then that was gone too. The nurse was herding everyone else into the waiting room. Looked like our moment alone was over.

"Let's go, babe," Mason said. "We need to catch a couple hours sleep before we meet the kids."

"Kids. Oh, is Misty back, then?" Jen asked.

"No," I said, maybe too quickly. "Jeremy and Christy are the kids. Misty too, when she gets back, and Josh, Jere's younger brother." I was explaining too much. I clamped my jaw to keep from saying anymore. It wasn't that I didn't trust Jen. She was one of those rare people I liked, but I wasn't going to admit to the local law that my niece had been at the scene of what had just become a homicide.

"You okay, Rachel?" Jen asked, coming closer.

"Yeah, I just... I almost feel for the guy. Maybe it's true that an unhappy life can't have a happy ending."

"Whoa, that's too deep for my oars," the Sheriff said. "There'll be an autopsy."

"About that," Mason said, and glanced at me. I nodded with my eyes. *I'm okay, go be a cop.* So he met the sheriff on the far end of the room, and said, "Let's get a coffee."

The two moved out of the waiting area back toward the lobby where we'd passed a coffee shop on the way in. I got up and started to follow, but my pace was slower.

Jen Scott fell into step alongside.

"What did you think about that head injury?" I asked Jen. I kept my eyes on my feet as we walked, closing off visual stimulation so I could try to feel her.

I had replayed every second of events in my mind, and she had been the only person alone outside that room. At least since we'd arrived. I couldn't be sure Paul hadn't died before that, though.

He'd probably just stopped breathing, like the nurse said. People do that after smoke inhalation. But something wasn't right. Something was itching at the base of my neck.

"I don't know," Jen said. "Maybe a beam fell on him, a

piece of furniture. Maybe he was stumbling around in the smoke and banged into something. I don't know. I don't know how the hell he got out, either."

"Through the bathroom window, I thought that's what Jeremy said."

"Said he found him on the ground outside there, yes. But there was no fire damage to the bathroom. He had all those burns on his lower legs, had inhaled smoke, had his head caved-in, and somehow he managed to get into the bathroom, close the door behind him, shove a wet towel under the door, open the window, and climb out."

I shrugged. "It's one for the books, all right. They can put it right beside the mom who picks up a flipped minivan off her trapped kid. It happens."

"It happens," she said. "For sure. I had a case where a sixty-pound lab dragged his two-hundred-fifteen-pound owner two miles through thick forest to a road where a passerby stopped to help. The guy's blood sugar had crashed, and he was in shock. Freaking dog saved his life."

I raised my hand, palm-up. "That's what I'm saying."

"Some people just don't want to die, I guess."

"I think when it's your time, it's your time. And when it's not, it's not." I was quoting directly from my own self-help books. "I think there's something bigger than us involved in all that."

She frowned at me. "You really believe that stuff you write about, don't you?"

I looked at her in surprise.

"Oh, yeah, I looked you up. I even started reading *Life is What You Make it*. 'There's a reason for everything. You just can't see some of those reasons from here.' Good stuff. Uplifting. I like it."

"Thanks. I appreciate that."

"'A reason for everything,'"

"I mean, I didn't invent that. They've been saying it for, you know, ever."

"Yeah, but the way you explained it..." She nodded slow as if she was still mulling the book, and okay, I was a sucker for an ego stroke, same as the next writer. She pulled out her phone and looked at its face. "I have to go. The chief is demanding an accounting. See you tomorrow."

"Yeah, tomorrow."

She left. I texted Christy to tell her that her sister was okay, and on her way there. And then I waited for Mason to finish his talk with Sheriff Rasmussen and kept an eye out for the dead guy's ghost.

CHRISTY

She was curled on the sofa in her aunt and uncle's romantic love nest, with hot cocoa and a warm, heavy bulldog snoring beside her. It was sweet, how in love those two were. She didn't think she would ever have a relationship like that. Mostly, she didn't think she wanted one.

Aunt Rache had texted her that Misty was okay and on her way there, but that her phone was dead so she couldn't text herself. Relief had surged, a warm rush of gratitude that her sister was okay— and a smaller one that she'd never have to put on a mermaid tail again.

Someone tapped the door, and a muffled voice called out.

"Misty?" She yanked her feet out from under the dog, who barely flinched, and ran to fling open the door. A bag went over her head, and the inside smelled... the inside smelled... oh hell, she was going to pass out...

JEREMY

When Jeremy got to the motel, he was exhausted. The whole drive he'd been playing out mind movies in which he was exposed for covering up his girlfriend's involvement in a crime.

He wouldn't have done anything differently, though.

He pulled up to the spot in front of door number six, but another car was in it. Misty's Jeep. And the light in the room was on. Please let her be ready to talk, he thought. This "break" was killing him.

She and Zig had stopped at an all-night diner for food, and she'd called him from a payphone there to tell him she wasn't going to Mason and Rachel's rental, but to a Saratoga Springs motel, and she would text him which one and the room number as soon as she checked in and plugged in her phone. She was dropping Zig at their dorm.

That kiss earlier... that had sparked something inside him. It hadn't felt like they'd gone back to normal, it felt like they'd elevated to a whole new level. But maybe that was just him. They hadn't talked.

He got out of the car and went to the door. She'd left the flip-lock open, so he could walk right in. She was sitting up on the bed with a bowl of pretzels, raisins and nuts in front of her. The light from the TV screen painted her face and long golden hair, still damp from a shower, in shifting light as she smiled a welcome and got to her feet.

"I thought you and Zig had to decompress."

"First we decamped— in record time, without our flashlights, so the cops and firefighters wouldn't see us in the woods." She came a few steps closer. "What went on back there?"

He lowered his head, moved farther inside, closed the door, and took off his jacket. "Uncle Mace just texted. Paul Quaid didn't make it."

"Oh, no!" Her eyes went wide as she said it, then shuttered as she said it again, "Oh, no," softer this time.

"I know. I um... I cleaned off the worst of the soot at the ER, but I'm in desperate need of a shower, and then we can—"

"I sorry for hurting you!" she blurted. "I only broke up with you because I didn't want to drag you into this mess, and now I've dragged you into it anyway, and it's a murder investigation now, and..." Her eyes were blue and wet and tired. "I don't know what to do."

"Nothing," he said. "It's done. We'll see it through to the end. You were one of the victims here, Misty. You could've died in that fire, too." His voice broke on those words. "I could make a case that I was afraid the killer would come for you if it got out you were there."

"But you lied to your own fellow cops."

"I don't know them. Detective Scott, Sheriff Rasmussen. I decided it was safer to trust no one." He shrugged one shoulder and said, "That's pretty much the truth anyway."

"Other than that Zig and I stalked the guy for two days until he finally left, then broke into his house to take pictures of his shi—" She bit off the rest.

"You took pictures of his shit?"

She blinked, "We, um—"

"You delete them yet?"

"They aren't digital— I mean, what are you— dammit, Jere, this is why I had to break it off. I don't want to have to lie to you, but I can't share everything with you either."

"I'm on your side, here! Did I not just put my ass on the line to cover for you?"

"Oh, and you're gonna throw that in my face for the next twenty years?" She pivoted, put her back to him and huffed.

"I was thinking more like the next sixty," he said, real softly. And then he wondered what demon had made him say it.

She turned around slow, blinking at him with Disney princess eyes. Yeah, he'd said it. Worse, he'd meant it. Son of a gun.

"I'm your guy, Misty. I've got your back. Right or wrong, good or bad, I've got you. So tell me what the hell is going on, already."

She took a deep breath, closed her eyes. "I love you," she

said. "But I can't. Not yet, I mean. It's not just me. I have a partner."

"You're partners with Zig in the podcast," he said, nodding slowly.

"Yeah. And... I love it. I love investigating, I love writing the scripts. I love all of it. I think it's what I want to do. I mean, really *do*."

He frowned and looked at her. Her eyes kind of sparkled when she talked about this thing.

"Just let me talk to Zig first, okay? I'll convince her we can trust you and then I'll tell you everything we have."

He wanted to agree. He didn't want to fight with her. "There's a killer on the loose. If you're withholding evidence—"

"I'll talk to her first thing in the morning. We'll talk to her together."

He closed his eyes. "Okay."

She sighed and he thought her tense muscles unclenched a little.

"All right. Then go take your shower and get back here already."

He raised his brows. "Because our break is truly over?"

"If you still want it to be. I wouldn't blame you if you—"

He crossed the room and kissed her before she could finish the sentence.

She laughed against his mouth and kissed him back. He'd never been so relieved in his life. "I love you," he said, wrapping her up and kissing her again and again. "I love you more than I even knew."

When he finally stopped, she had tears on her cheeks. "Go take your shower."

He kissed her once more, then headed into the bathroom. On the way in he heard her phone chirp. He hurried through his shower, eager for the making up part of their breakup.

When he came back out, she was gone.

Her car was gone. Her phone was gone. Jeremy swallowed hard, grabbed his phone, texted Misty.

> Jeremy: What happened?

> Misty: Meeting Christy. Sorry. She needed me.

So did I, he thought, and the voice in his head sounded like a whiny shit, even to him. Misty and Christy were more than sisters. They were twins. They would always be number one to each other. And he didn't think he'd want it to be different.

> Jeremy: Let me know if I can help.

She didn't reply, so he curled up on the bed to wait and eventually he fell asleep.

When he woke, the sun was beaming in on his face and Misty still wasn't back.

RACHEL

Christy's car was in the driveway. Our headlights spilled across it as we pulled into our home away from home.

But I didn't see the Firebird or Misty's Jeep.

As soon as we got out of the car, I heard Myrtle's snuffly version of a bark from inside the house, and I ran up the front steps. Over and over, she yipped. The front door was unlocked. It opened when I twisted, and Myrt was on the other side, yipping over and over, with so much force her front paws came off the floor.

I turned to Mason. "Something's wrong. Find Christy!"

He ran past me, up the stairs, and I heard doors slamming and his steps pounding from room to room. I gathered my trembling bulldog into my arms and lifted all sixty pounds of her. "It's okay, baby. I've got you. Everything's okay."

Mason came running down the stairs and surged through the rest of the house and out the back door. I carried Myrtle through to the master bedroom, where her big, fluffy cushion was already on the bed, and I set her there and pet her and soothed her as best I could while shaking myself.

Mason came back into the room. "She's not here. But her car is. So that means someone else took her," Mason said.

"It might've been Misty and Jeremy. They're both MIA too."

"They were getting a motel room," Mason said.

"Wow. Okay, thanks for telling me."

"He confided in me. What was I gonna do?"

"She wouldn't have left Myrtle alone. And you saw Myrt, she was traumatized."

He pulled out his phone. "I'm calling Jen Scott."

I put my hand over his. "I can't read her, you know."

"Yeah, you said..." He trailed off, searched my eyes.

"She was alone outside Quaid's hospital room. Not for long, but—"

"You don't think..."

"That dog tag thing has been niggling at me. It means Paul Quaid was in the military. And didn't that first episode of Misty and Zig's podcast say Jen Scott was ex-military?"

"Explosives ordinance specialist," Mason said slowly. "You think they served together?"

"Maybe more than served together?" I asked.

"It's all speculation. We don't have any evidence. We could find it though." He picked up his phone and made a call. While he waited for an answer, he said, "It's okay. We'll find her. We will."

MISTY

The text came through while her phone was plugged in. Jeremy was in the shower. She heard it running and her heart squeezed. They were back together. They were okay.

She looked at her phone and saw Christy's face, glanced at the message to see what her sister was up to, then went ice cold inside.

Christy: I have your sister. Come alone or she dies. Tell your boyfriend and she dies. I have eyes on you. Leave now. Head north. Ten seconds. Be in your car in ten seconds.

She sprang from the bed, looking around frantically.

Christy: 9.

Christy: 8.

"Shit!" She grabbed her bag, her shoes, and her keys, and dashed out the door juggling them.

Christy: 5.

Christy: 4.

She yanked open the Jeep's door, slinging her shoes and purse onto the passenger seat, jamming her foot on the brake, and poking the start button. She didn't even have the door shut as she reversed all the way into the road and jammed it into drive.

Christy: 3, 2, 1.

She pressed her thumb onto the mic icon, and said, "I'm fucking going already, Jesus fucking Christ!" and tapped send.

Then the car's computer voice said, "Keep going north. I'll tell you went to get off," and she jumped so high she hit the ceiling. The phone had connected, as it always did. She just hadn't been expecting it to start reading the texts aloud.

She looked into the rearview mirror. There were no cars behind her. One was coming from the opposite direction though, its headlights shining in her eyes. She looked down at herself. She wore short yoga pants and a T-shirt with elaborately decorated cupcakes all over it, and the caption, "I baked you some shutthefuckupcakes." It had been a gift from Aunt Rachel.

She bit her lip. She ought to call Aunt Rache, if no-one else. There was no way that person could know.

Or could they? Her phone had been out of her possession for a while. What if someone had duped it or bugged it? What if they were tracking every screen-touch?

How the hell was the person watching her?

They weren't. They said they were, but they'd kept counting after she'd already started the car.

She took the phone, texting with one thumb as fast as she could've spoken it.

Misty: What now?

No reply. The white lines were blurring together, so she eased up on the accelerator, backed the needle down from 89 to 80. Then she picked up the phone again, scrolled to contacts, scrolled to Aunt Rachel. Tapped her image.

The phone pinged in her hand. "Don't," it said aloud, scaring her so bad she dropped the phone onto the floor. When she reached for it, she veered off the road, onto the shoulder, then jerked the car the other way. The rear-end fish-tailed. She clasped the wheel with both hands and the phone, swearing more than she ever had in her life.

She got under control, breathed fast. Then she skimmed the car's interior. There had to be a camera somewhere, didn't there?

"Take the next right," said Siri.

"You're taking me to the club?" she asked, and the phone transcribed. "Send."

"Be here in five. Come in the back way, and don't do anything stupid. I'll know. She'll die." Somehow the inflectionless computer voice made the chills down her spine even colder.

Taking the exit, Misty pressed the pedal to the floor, then skidded into the parking lot without bothering to choose a space. She exited where the car landed, but she didn't go inside. She tapped Christy's number to call her.

It only rang once. Then someone picked up but didn't say anything.

"I want to talk to my sister," she said.

From a distance, she heard, "Misty, don't come in here! She'll just kill us both if you—"

The call ended.

Misty was out of the car, and the air was like a cold slap in the face. Dawn was still hours away. Three, maybe.

If there had been a camera on her, it had to be in the car. It had been parked at the far side of the woods the whole time they'd been watching Paul Quad's cabin, in a pull-off used by hikers. Anyone could've got in. Locked, yes, but still... She held her phone face-up but kept her arm at her side and she scrolled to Aunt Rachel's contact card while she walked up the back stairs. They rattled and clanged with every step, no matter how quiet she tried to be. She tapped share location on her phone, then quickly closed out of the app and silenced it.

She'd reached the top of the back stairs. There was a ledge above the door a couple of inches wide. Part of the wood trim. She put the phone up there, face-in. Its case was brown pleather. It blended right in.

Okay. She took a deep breath, grabbed the doorknob, and went inside.

Christy was on the floor beside the tank. She didn't know where the killer was, but Detective Jen Scott was right there, too, and she had her gun out.

"Thank god," she said, but then she noticed how terrified Christy looked, and realized Jen Scott was pointing the gun at her.

"Put on your fins," she said. "Time to take one last swim."

"I don't understand," Christy said from the floor. She was wearing her bra on top, that stupid mermaid thing Mom had got them on a chain around her neck, and a blue tail that went from powder blue at the waist, shifting through every shade, to midnight blue edged in silver at the tail.

God, that was Eva's tail, Misty realized. She'd seen it a hundred times in the photo. Detective Scott hadn't even been on her radar.

"Where did you get Eva's tail?" Misty asked, her voice shaking.

"Didn't you hear? They found her body. Well, I found her body. First, I dumped it, and then I found it. Didn't plan it that way, but..." She frowned for a moment. "She washed right up in our spot. Like she came back for me." And then her face twisted, and she said, "She was still so beautiful."

"Jesus fucking Christ," Christy said, grimacing at the tail she'd been forced to wear. "How do you think killing us is going to help you, lady? There are more than just the two of us digging into this. You know that, right?"

"She's right. Killing us will make them dig all the harder," Misty said. She was still standing with her back to the door. She noticed the pool-cover mechanism on the floor, leaning crookedly against the wall with its wires stretched upward.

"Your auntie and uncle will be dead before you are," Jen said. "That only leaves your boyfriend— the rookie, and you know, suicide *is* the leading cause of death among police officers. And then the Ziglar girl. An accident for her, I think." Jen strode over to where Christy lay on the floor, grabbed her by her hair, and jammed the gun to her temple so hard she yelped in pain. "Get into costume. Now."

"Okay, okay!" Misty screamed. "Jesus stop hurting her you sick fuck!" All as she hurried to where Jen had pointed. A costume bag lay on the bench. She unzipped it and saw a getup she'd never seen before. The tail was palest pink at the waist, gradually darkening to vivid hot pink at the tail. It was stunning. The top had pink shells over fabric that was ingeniously concealed. She then unzipped the tail and got into it, facedown, moving slowly, watching her sister's eyes the whole time.

Get the hell out of here. Get help. Or we're both dead. That's what her sister's eyes were telling her. She didn't doubt it. She didn't want to leave.

Christy's eyes flared wider. *It's our only chance.*

Jen stood over her head, her gun still pointed. "Hand me your string."

235

Misty pushed her butt out to make the zipping harder as Jen tugged with one arm, keeping the gun pointed with the other.

"This isn't going to work," she said. "I don't know what you were talking about before, but Rachel and Mason are on their way here."

Jen dropped the pull string in frustration. "I know. I counted on it. But they won't make it here." She smiled and made kaboom fingers on either side of her head.

Misty frowned, and then remembered. *Detective Jen Scott, former Army explosives ordinance specialist...* The words of her own script came to her.

Jen Scott bent low to resume tugging on the zipper.

"Detective, wait," Misty said. "There's one more thing."

Jen Scott sent her a scorching look. "*What?*"

"Mermaid Pose!" Misty straightened her arms, arched her back, and smashed her head into Jen's face. Then she rolled onto her back, yanked her legs out of the tail, and dashed for the back door.

"I'll shoot your sister!" Jen screamed as she lurched to her feet.

"No, she fucking won't!" Christy yelled, and then there was a splash. She'd gone into the water.

Misty lurched through the door, slammed it behind her, grabbed her phone and tapped the mic, screaming "Text Rachel. Bomb in car!"

The door slammed into her from behind, and she flew forward, shouting "Send! *Send!*" Her phone sailed into the air as she fell. But what she heard was even worse; the screechy grinding sound of the motor closing the pool cover. Jen had thrown the lever before coming after her!

Then came the first impact of her body against the staircase, followed by many others as the world spun around her, pounding her the whole time.

RACHEL

As soon as Christy had shared her location, Mason and I had jumped into action. We took Myrtle with us, in the back seat of the car. She'd be more comfortable than in a strange house all alone. The car was her favorite place, familiar and safe.

Mason drove, I navigated, but after the first two turns, I said, "It's gotta be the club. She's at The Sapphire Club." And in my mind's eye, I saw Eva Quaid, as mermaid Esmeralda, pounding the glass of the aquarium, her eyes round and brown and pleading.

"Faster, Mason."

He pressed the accelerator. We were nearly there when my phone lit up again.

Christy: Bomb in car.

"Stop the car!" I shrieked. Then, "No, drive out into that field first. Hurry! But gently. But hurry." I climbed over into the back seat and scooped up my dog.

Mason looked at me like I'd lost my mind, but he found a

tractor path into the field I'd indicated and drove over it, leaving the pavement behind.

The car bounded and I said, "Easy. A little farther. Hurry! But easy. There's a bomb in the car, I think."

The car bounced to a stop. "Far enough," he said. "I've got your phone. Head for the road. Ready?"

I grabbed my backpack, gave a nod. We got out in unison, then ran back toward the road. Mason came to take Myrtle from my arms. I could move way faster without her. We jumped the ditch, crossed the road, went down the little slope on the other side and then crouched arm-in-arm with Myrt between us, peering back.

Nothing happened.

"Huh," I said. "Maybe I was wro—"

The blast shattered my ears and the yellow-white flash blinded me. Then the percussion hit me in the face, and I went over backwards and down the little slope. I tried to say "Holy fuck" but I didn't have any breath in my lungs.

Then Mason was pulling me up into his arms as a car went speeding by.

"Oh, don't even stop, you mother fucker!" I shouted with both birds aloft. But then I put my arms back around Mason and held on tight. Myrtle was sitting right where we'd left her. Poor dog.

"You okay?" Too soon he pulled away enough to look me over.

I nodded. "You?"

"Yeah."

I heaved a big sigh, then said, "Jen Scott was an Army

explosives specialist," I said. "Remember that? It was in the first episode."

"Yeah, and I had an email from my friend in military records. Jen Scott and Paul Quaid served in the same unit at the same time."

I looked around, spotted my phone and backpack a few feet apart on the slope, and went to get them. Then I returned to Myrtle and sat down beside her. Mason joined us and I showed him the message from Misty.

"Text her back," he said. "I'll get help."

I texted Christy. "We're ok. Where are you? How did you know?"

But she didn't reply.

"Try Misty," he said.

"I cc'd her. Neither of them are responding. Mason, I'm scared. Something's wrong, something's really fucking wrong. We have to find them."

He called Jeremy on speaker, and Jere picked up on the first ring.

"Thank God," I said.

Mason said, "Jere, we think someone took Christy from the house."

"Jesus," he said. "Misty left while I was in the shower. Said her sister needed her, so I assumed she was there with you."

"We think they're at the club. We're on the road to it, a mile and half out."

"I'll meet you there."

"We're fine, Jeremy," Mason said, "But someone blew up our car. We're stranded on the roadside."

"What the— I'll pick you up."

"No, go straight to the club," I said. "We called the state police first, and I can already hear sirens. Don't stop for us, in case we get hung up with them."

"Phone-finder says they were both at the club before Misty's phone went offline," Mason added. "We'll meet you there."

"On my way," he said.

With Myrtle at my feet, I waved my arms at the police car. There were two others behind it, and an ambulance to boot. When a cop called in, there was a response. Badge out, Mason went up to the first cop who arrived.

"Detective Brown! Holy, hell," said the officer, holding out a hand. "Sergeant Jarrod Kenner."

"Sergeant Kenner." Mason shook, but the cop was looking toward the still blazing car.

"How the hell did you survive?"

"Somebody tipped us off," Mason said, "and she might be in danger. We can't reach her."

"You know where she is?"

"Yes, but we need a ride."

Kenner led them to the second car that had stopped, with its driver still behind the wheel, though his door was open. "Asher you're in charge of the scene," Sergeant Kenner said, then he turned to Mason. "Anything else?"

"Yeah, let's keep this on the QT until further notice. No press. No leaks. No idea what happened here or whether anyone was in the car at the time."

Kenner nodded. "Play dumb. Got it, Asher?"

"Got it, Sarge."

The sergeant led us to his car and opened his door. "Hop in, I'll drive."

Mason opened the passenger side, front, and offered it to me.

"I'll take the back." I opened the door but before I got in, Mason picked up Myrt and set her in before me.

She sighed and laid down. It wasn't her car, but it was a car. The sarge handed me a dewy water bottle over the seat. "Thanks. I need that." I took a drink, then poured some into my palm and offered it to Myrt. She took a couple of licks, then declined, so I wiped the rest onto my jeans.

We took off with lights and siren on full tilt.

I took another drink, lowered the bottle and saw Eva, the dead mermaid inside. She flipped her tail and splashed water straight up out of the bottle and into my face, making me yelp in shock.

Both men turned sharply.

"Leg cramp," I said. And of course, my face was dry.

But Mason kept his eyes on me after that.

The mermaid was still in the bottle, shaking her hands and shouting words I couldn't hear. "I think we should hurry."

CHAPTER 13

CHRISTY

Christy couldn't get out of the cool, chlorinated water before the pool cover closed. She didn't even swim all the way up, but stopped where she was, staring up as the last inch of light vanished from the water's the surface.

God, it was Detective Jen Scott. *She* had killed Eva. But why? And where the hell was Jen now, and where was Misty? She'd made a run for it, but Christy had a bad feeling.

Be okay, Misty. Be strong. Be smart. Survive.

Her heart was racing. She needed to breathe!

She told herself not to panic and swam down to the nearest flower, turned the valve and inhaled precious air. Relief surged through her. Until there was no more. The air supply just ended.

God, Jen had turned off the oxygen!

Christy flipped to another air flower, and another,

sucking desperately at each hose, gathering what little oxygen remained trapped in its length, and no more.

Through the front of the tank, she could see the empty dining room, the bar. No signs of life. There was no one in the darkened private room off the side wall, either. But Eva was there. Her photo was there on the wall, her face waving behind the water's gentle, deadly motion.

Oh, God. Oh, God she was going to die in this freaking pool! And she knew with sudden clarity that Eva Quaid had died there, too.

MISTY

Misty woke and raised her arms over her face only to slam them into the ceiling. *Ohmygod I'm in a coffin!* She started pounding, breathing too fast, panicking.

Be okay, Misty. Be strong. Be smart. Survive. It was Christy's voice whispering through her mind. As if she knew.

Misty grabbed hold of her panic and, as soon as she did, she realized she was moving. She was in a car. Right, the trunk of a car.

That was so much better than a coffin.

She felt around for a trunk release. Some cars had them, but she figured Jen Scott would know whether hers did. She'd been driving an ancient Bronco that day she'd come to the club. This was a different vehicle.

She didn't expect to find a release, and she didn't. But she knew the deal. She'd had a cop for an uncle since she was sixteen. So she started poking around the edges of the carpet that lined the trunk, finding a corner she could pry back and working on that. Everyone knew to punch out a taillight and stick out your hand.

The damn carpet wasn't coming up easily. She suddenly wished she had that stupid tool thing her mom had sent her.

Mom. God, she'd been so proud of those damn things. Tears came when she thought of her mother, and she closed her eyes and immediately saw Christy, holding her ugly metal mermaid in her hand.

It made her slide her hand into her jacket pocket, where it closed around her own silly metal mermaid. Hell, she'd forgotten putting it there. And for some reason she pulled it out and draped its chain around her neck.

Something felt wrong and she whispered. "Are you okay, Sis?"

The carpet she was pulling at came loose so fast she fell backward and banged her head. She rubbed the spot and sucked air through her teeth. When she could move again, she felt around for the taillight, but there was a whole metal cup that held it, and a bunch of wires coming out the back. She started trying to feel around the edges of the metal thingy, and then she gave up and just started shoving it. She wished she could kick it out, but she didn't think there was room in the trunk to turn around. She was already feeling a little claustrophobic and if she got stuck halfway, she'd lose it for sure.

The car hit a bump and her body bounced right off the floor and smashed into the lid. Shit, they'd gone off-road.

And they were still moving, bounding and bouncing like mad.

She turned toward the one area she hadn't explored, the part that separated the trunk from back seat. And then she turned sideways, in spite of it being cramped as hell, she kicked with both feet and all her strength.

The seat shot forward, and she scrambled into the car. Then as Jen turned around and saw her, she moved as far to the passenger side as she could. Jen reached back for her, one hand on the wheel while the car veered wildly. Misty had to jam her hand between the tipped over seat-back and the door to get hold of its handle.

Locked. She unlocked it manually. Jen caught a handful of her long hair, but Misty got the door open, and kicked Jen in the face to propel herself out of the car. The ground hit her as hard as those stairs had, all the way down, and her body tumbled in much the same way. She had no control. She just rolled until she didn't.

The car skidded to a stop ahead. It was pitch dark. They were in a field. Misty pushed herself to her feet but stayed low and moved silently, scanning her surroundings in search of a place to hide. There was a sound. Rushing water.

"Come back here, Goddamn you!" Jen Scott shouted. Her voice echoed in the vast darkness.

Noise was good, Misty thought. The sound of the water would cover any sound she made. So she headed for it. It led her to the road, or rather to the culvert that went underneath the road. The field ended in an upward slope to the road, with a big round tunnel bored through it. Lined in concrete, the culvert allowed water to run beneath the road. It wasn't much water just then, a skinny strand a couple of inches deep. The tunnel was big enough for a cow to pass through.

Jen was tramping through the field, swinging a flashlight, and Misty ducked into the tall grasses and weeds.

She thought it would make sense to head for the road and try to find help. But she knew that was the most obvious move she could make. So instead, she decided to cross the road through the culvert and see what was on the other side.

Misty stepped into the water, and then entered the darkest dark of her entire life.

RACHEL

The whole way, panic had been wrapping its adrenaline fingers around my heart. I kept forgetting to breathe, and then suddenly gasping like a suffocating fish. I saw the looks the state cop kept sending Mason. So did Mason, but he was pretending not to.

Finally, the vehicle bounded into the driveway of the club and skidded sideways near the front entrance.

I grabbed my door handle and yanked it so hard I about broke my damn hand. Locked. "Fucking open the goddamn—"

Mason was out and yanking the door open before the trooper even got his siren turned off. Then he lunged to the club's front entrance and got there before me. I expected him to kick it in, but he just opened it. Unlocked.

We ran inside and stopped, looking around. The curtain was raised. And something was moving inside the dark aquarium. "It's Christy!" I knew it in my heart, I didn't need to see her.

We ran to the tank, but it was too dark. Oddly dark. Something was in the back, near those fake flowers. I knew two things instantly. "Christy's in the tank! Mason, the cover is closed!"

Mason raced to the stair door, grabbing the trooper by the arm on the way. I heard them thunder up the stairs, heard them shouting.

The tank lights came on.

Christy had been sucking at one of the flowers that spouted oxygen, but she spotted me and swam to the glass, pressing her hands to it, shaking her head no.

"Mason!" I screamed.

"Trying! The motor's gone!"

I looked around, grabbed a chair, and swung it into the tank for all I was worth. It hit and the recoil spun me the other way and about ripped out my shoulder, but I came right back around, swinging again, and then again.

Not even a crack. "*Mason!*" I shrieked.

Jeremy came in, ran up behind me. "I don't have my sidearm!" he cried. "Christy!"

I met Christy's eyes. She was terrified, I could see her chest spasming for air and bouncing that stupid thing Sandra had bought her and—

"The Crisis Companion!" I yelled, and then I grabbed at my necklace, held it up and pointed to hers.

She got it. I saw hope in her eyes and she grabbed the

thing, picking it up, turning it frantically, and finally pressing its tip against the glass of the tank just as the cop reached my side, with his gun drawn to shoot out the glass.

"Wait!" I dashed sideways as a sort of after-thought, but it was too late. I heard a gentle, *tink*. Then the tank exploded.

Hell, I should've thought to get out of the way, huh? A wall of water with big sharp glass shards carried me and the tables and the chairs all the way to the entry doors, and I was jammed up against them, back-first, trying to get a breath while water blasted my face. My hands fumbled over my head, found the handle, and the doors swung open. I whooshed right through along with gallons and gallons of water.

Finally, the water sluiced away, leaving me gasping at the bottom of the stairs. "Christy!" I scrambled to push myself upright but my hands were slick, because my arm was bleeding so much. I found the cut, clasped it with my other hand, and got to my feet limping back inside. "Christy!"

She was lying facedown in the water, just the same way she'd been lying in the water in my dream. She was near the front wall where we'd sat that first night in the place. When I saw her there, her position, the curve of her arm, the water sluicing from her body, that nightmare vision of her flashed in my mind. Identical. It was identical...

...except for the slow flip of her mermaid tail.

"Christy!" Shaking away my paralyzing fear, I fell down beside her, gathering her up and hugging her to my chest. She was all right. She was okay. I held her while I looked for Jeremy. Then I spotted him. He was pushing himself up amid a pile of toppled tables and chairs over by the door Mason had just come through, and gave him a hand up on the way by.

"Get me out of this tail, will you Aunt Rache?"

I nodded. Christy rolled onto her belly, and I got the zipper down. I helped her peel the thing off without getting her silky leggings wet. They were the only dry thing on her. Then she sprang to her feet and right into my arms. "I thought that was it. I really thought that was it!"

"I know," I said. "I know, but you're okay." I pushed her wet hair off her face. "Thank God, you're okay. Where is Misty?"

"With Jen Scott!" She sort of yelled it, pulling out of my embrace. "Aunt Rache, that detective is the bad guy!"

"She didn't *find* the body," Mason said. "She planted it."

"No, she *did* find it, she told us so. She said she dumped the body, and then she found it, and that Eva had found her way to *their spot*."

"It was *their* spot," I whispered.

Mason went on. "She planted Paul Quaid's dog tag to frame him, then killed him so he couldn't deny it."

I blinked as my brain filled in blanks. "She's been pretending to help us just to keep track of what we knew, what we were looking at," I said. "And to subtly steer us toward Paul."

"Paul was investigating too," Jeremy said. He went to his backpack. "Zig got the photos they took at Quaid's cabin digitized last night and sent them to me when I told her Misty was missing."

He pulled up the photos taken inside the Quaid house before it had burned, then turned his phone our way.

The first photo was of a corkboard wall covered in other photos, clippings, and handwritten notes. I swiped through closeups of several of the items pinned to the board. One was a photo of two young women, arm in arm. I recognized them both. One was Eva Quaid. They were arm in arm, smiling at each other in a way only lovers do.

"They were together," Jeremy said real slow. "And she told us she was the one who introduced Eva to Paul."

"So, Paul fell for Eva," I said. "And Eva married him. And Jen killed them both for it."

"And planned to kill us, too. We have to find Misty." There were tears around the edges of Christy's voice. "We have to."

"How the hell did you break that glass?" Jeremy asked. He bent to pick up a piece. "Look how thick it is."

Christy wrapped her hand around the giant, ugly thing hanging from a chain around her neck and said, "Crisis Companion. An innocent young woman's best friend in the cold, cruel world." She held it up, spokesmodel style, complete with big smile, but then the smile dissolved in the tears that streamed down her face. "My fuckin' mother. You tell her and I'll never hear the end of it."

"You *shouldn't* ever hear the end of it," I said. "It saved your perky ass. You should be on your knees thanking her."

"I know." She sighed. "Misty ran out the upper stair door, right after Jen said you two would never make it here alive," Christy said. "I assumed she was going to try to warn you."

"She texted us just in time," I said. "Jen had planted a bomb in our car."

"She hit the cover lever, then went after Misty," Christy

went on. "The control box was off the wall, propped up on the floor, wires showing. I noticed just as I dove in."

"She must've brought it in with her," I said.

"And she took it with her when she left," Mason added.

The cover closed before I could get back up," Christy said. Her voice was pitching up a little. "The air tanks were turned off. Jen and Misty never came back."

"We'll find her in time," I said. I put my hands on her shoulders, and she surprised me by falling right into my arms and sobbing. "I promise, we will. But I have to call your mother and fill her in. She'll kill me for not telling her sooner."

"I'll do it," Christy said. She closed her hand around the metal mermaid on her chest. "I owe her one."

"You owe her all of them, kid."

MISTY

Crouching in the far end of the sluice pipe where there was barely enough light from a sliver of moon to see by, Misty fumbled with that stupid Crisis Companion her mother had sent her. She'd totally forgotten that she'd shoved it into her jacket pocket and now she was trying to see what miraculous rescue it had to offer. A phone, maybe? She'd seen it in her sister's hand, very clearly. It must mean something.

She recalled its enclosed flyer touting the device's

features: seatbelt slicer, mini-can of pepper spray, rape whistle, and that windshield-breaker.

She hadn't had one of those odd spasms in her chest for several minutes, and pressed her hands there, closing her eyes and whispering her sister's name. Christy was no longer gasping for air.

Which either meant she was okay, or she was dead.

Misty closed her eyes and everything in her wept. The very core of her twisted into a knot. But the devastating thought was just that— a thought. Not a feeling. Her only sensation was relief that the spasms in her chest had ended.

"Be okay, be okay, be okay."

"Where are you, you little shit?" Jen Scott called.

Misty clapped a hand over her mouth, realizing she'd whispered aloud. Her eyes wide, she cast them back down the tunnel. She was crouching near the opening on the far side. Beyond, there was a hundred-foot clearing, backed by a wall of trees. Maybe a forest.

Should I head for the woods? Might be easier to hide. But I'd have to cross all that open space, and she'd see me for sure.

She looked back up the tunnel. A beam of light appeared, and she gasped behind her hand. It was Jen Scott's flashlight, waving back and forth across the weed and wildflower field beyond the culvert's entrance. Misty thought she had probably trampled down grasses on the way in. It had been ass-high. She'd probably left a clear trail.

"Nobody's coming to save you, Misty. There's nobody left to save you."

Oh, God, what did that mean? Was Christy dead? Had she

done something to Jeremy, too? Had Rachel and Mason got her text in time? Had she even sent it? Misty's mind was spiraling.

And then suddenly, *Fuck that crazy bitch.*

Christy. She had just felt Christy inside her head. Or channeled her in that way that happened with the two of them sometimes. It had always. When one was in some kind of stressful situation, the other's voice would just pop in. Sometimes the other twin was aware of it, sensing it, and other times it happened without them even knowing. Consciously, at least.

Jen was getting closer. Misty had to make a decision. And her feeling that her sister was okay helped her find the will to get up and move again.

The flashlight beam came into the culvert. Decision made. Misty scurried out the opening and quickly ducked to the left. Hugging the grassy mound beside the opening, she leaned in just enough to see the light beam shining from the other end, sweeping the inside, and she jerked her head back out of the way.

Then the beam left the culvert. On her belly, Misty scooted up to road-height and peered across. Jen came striding up from the other side, her light sweeping up and down the pavement.

Misty ducked, then scrambled right back inside the culvert and moved as fast as she could back to the entrance, praying the running water would cover the sounds of her feet moving through it. She ducked out the same way she'd come in, once again crouching to the side to wait, watch, and listen.

Jen shone her light into the culvert from the far end, even

walked in a little ways. Misty pressed her back to the cool, sloping ground beside the opening, waiting. She heard Jen sigh. It echoed in the cavern. Then her feet sloshed water a few times and then the culvert went silent.

Misty closed her eyes and had a vision of running back to where Jen had left her car and finding it with the keys still inside. She would take it and go find her family.

When she thought enough time had passed, she pushed up to her feet, and started back the way she'd come, toward Jen Scott's car.

"There you are."

Misty spun around so fast she wrenched her neck and saw Jen Scott standing in the mouth of the culvert, holding a handgun pointed right at her.

"This is the perfect spot."

A hammer hit her in the chest. The sound of the gunshot followed, but Misty was already on the ground by the time she heard it. Her eyes were wide. The sky was full of stars. She hadn't even noticed them. She couldn't remember the last time she had. There were so many!

Footsteps in the grasses. She closed her eyes, or she hoped she did. She told her eyes to close, but it seemed like communication between her mind and her body had been cut off. She couldn't feel anything. No pain, which was good, and not even the chilly night air.

Then there was a sensation— movement, and a tug near her scalp, then harder. Jen was dragging her by her ponytail. What a shitty thing to do. It should probably hurt more.

There was cold and wet on her back. The culvert. Jen was dragging her inside. And then she stopped and Misty heard,

"It's too bad, blondie. You weren't a bad mermaid. Nothing like Eva, but still."

She dragged her a little farther, then let go of her hair. Misty lay faceup in the icy, shallow water, willing her eyes not to flutter and her muscles not to shiver.

"The coyotes'll take care of your body before anyone ever looks way the hell out here," Jen Scott went on. "I kept Eva too long. Way too long. Not gonna make that mistake again. Or any others. I have two loose ends left. I'm gonna turn on a phone and lure your rookie and your partner right up here where I want them. A little more food for the coyotes." She delivered a kick to Misty's side that flipped her right over, facedown in the water, and then as she sloshed away, "I think I've actually got this. Finally. It's almost over."

CHAPTER 14

RACHEL

We divided ourselves between Misty's Jeep and Jeremy's Firebird and headed back to the house where Christy's car awaited.

When we all got out, I said, "Christy and I need dry clothes—"

"You need your arm bandaged," Mason said.

"And Myrtle needs a walk, and food, and then bed with the TV on, and one of her four-hour dog chews. Did you bring some, Jere?"

"Of course I did," Jeremy replied. "I'll walk her while you change."

Mason nodded at him. "Did I hear you say you didn't bring your sidearm?"

"Yeah."

"I'll grab my spare for you." We walked inside, Mason

and I, to the master bedroom. I started trying to strip off my soaking wet clothes one-handed.

"Hey, hey," he said as I struggled. Then he took my blouse and pulled it over my head, dropped it on the floor, and walked me into the attached bathroom. He rummaged in the cabinet for bandages, found a nice roll of gauze, some thick pads, adhesive tape, and disinfectant, which he poured on the cut before I could pull away.

I hissed.

"Sorry," he said. Then he pressed on the thick pads and started wrapping.

"Hurry," I said. "We have to go after her."

"We don't know where to go." He finished wrapping and sealed the deal with several strips of tape. "There. You can get dressed now."

"Thanks." I headed back into the bedroom, located a clean pair of jeans, a sweater, thick socks, and a dry pair shoes. Then I grabbed my denim jacket. Mason was rummaging in the closet where he'd stashed his locked gun box as soon as we'd arrived, arming himself for whatever we were about to face.

Jeremy tapped on the door, and when Mason said, "Come," he entered with Myrtle at his side.

"Okay, good. Put her here." I patted the dog bed, atop the people bed, and I tuned the TV to animal planet.

She was exhausted from all the excitement, and I thought she'd sleep for a day. I just didn't know if she'd do it here. I left water and a long lasting chew and kissed her face. "I'll be back soon," I said.

Then I left and closed the door. She'd be fine.

She really will, Inner Bitch said.

Misty might not, though, I thought. I sensed clearly that the danger to Christy had passed, but my fear for Misty still lurked like a dark shadow behind my thoughts.

Minutes later, Christy came down the stairs in dry clothes, her phone in her hand. "Misty's phone is back online," she said, showing us the location app. I saw the little circle pinging from a dot on its screen. "She's not far. Let's go." She grabbed her keys and headed for the door.

"Wait a sec, wait a sec. Let me see that," Jeremy said.

Christy handed him the phone, but she was clearly eager to hit the road.

"It's north," he said. "In the middle of nowhere."

"All the more reason to hurry!" She grabbed the phone from his hand and headed for the door.

"It's a trap," Mason said. "Jen turned the phone off until she wanted us to know where it was, then she turned it back on."

I met Christy's questioning eyes and nodded. "He's right. But Jen Scott probably thinks Mason and I died when she blew up our car."

Jeremy said, "Yes, and she thinks Christy died in the tank. I'm the only one she expects to show up."

"That gives us an advantage," I said. "Let's use it wisely. All right?"

Everyone nodded and listened to the plan.

MISTY

Misty startled awake in a blaze of pain. Her cheek was ice cold from the water, but somehow she'd turned sideways enough not to drown. She couldn't move, but she could feel. Her head pulsed bigger and smaller inside her skull. Her body was ice cold and wet. She was blind. Or in total darkness. Or dead. No. Death wouldn't hurt like this. She couldn't be dead.

God, she didn't want to be dead.

She had to find her sister. She had to make sure Christy was okay. She had to finish making up with Jeremy. She had to finish the podcast. But she wasn't going to do any of that, was she? Because she was lying in a culvert in the middle of nowhere, shot in the chest, probably dying.

Dying. At twenty-two. She'd only just figured out what she wanted to do with the rest of her life. She wanted to spend it solving mysteries. And she wanted to spend it with Jeremy.

She closed her eyes and hot tears burned. She couldn't move. She couldn't even drag her body to the road where someone could find it and tell her family. She couldn't do anything but lie there in the freezing cold with her chest throbbing so hard it felt like her ribs were broken.

God, it hurt!

And then there was a sound she felt even more than she felt the pain; a distant warbling howl.

The coyotes will take care of the evidence. Jen Scott's disembodied voice rang through the culvert. And then it went on. *Only two loose ends left.*

She had to have been talking about Jeremy. Jeremy and Zig.

"Fuck that," she said. And then she forced her hands to move, her arms to move, and pushed herself up onto her side. It hurt, but she had to touch her chest, to feel the damage, to see...

She slid her hand over her heart, toward the center, and then felt metal. Metal embedded *in* her chest. She spread her palm out, tipped her head down, and saw most of it— that metal mermaid was sunken right into her flesh. She ran her fingers down its distorted shape, gently, because any pressure on it hurt like hell. And right in the middle, where the mermaid's waist met the top of her tail, there was a round, flattened disk of a different material. Lead, she thought.

"The bullet. The freaking bullet."

She took hold of the chain, and clenching her jaw, she pulled the metal mermaid out of her chest, and bit her lips so hard to keep from screaming that she tasted blood.

RACHEL

Misty's phone location was pinging to my phone as well as Jeremy's. He had his car, and I had Misty's Jeep. Christy was in the back seat, and Mason was driving while I navigated, using the map on his phone so I could keep the location app open on mine.

"Take a right up here, then the first left. That circles

around behind the phone's location. Jeremy's going straight in."

Mason took the turn, drove a little ways, then took the left. We drove between woodlands that fell away, revealing wide open meadows on either side of the road.

"The phone is out that way, in that field to the left," I said, pointing. "Keep driving past it, though."

Mason did, pulling over where the trees began once again, and then off the road a little ways, to make the car less obvious.

He got out, checked his gun, and didn't put it back in its holster. He was done fucking around.

My phone vibrated in my hand, and I looked down at it, then at my two companions. "It's Sandra," I said, "She and Jim have arrived at the house. They're with Myrtle and they want to know what's going on."

Christy snatched the phone from my hand and tapped a message back so fast it had to be some kind of supernatural ability. Then she handed it back to me, and I looked down to see "my" reply.

> Rachel: Everything is fine. We're picking up the girls and we'll be back in a couple of hours. Breakfast would be great.

I looked at her. "You said you were going to call her."

"I did."

"And?"

"And I told her to come out to the house you rented, and we'd spend the morning together." She shrugged. "We can tell them about all this later. Wouldn't do any good now."

I sighed and added a message of my own.

> Rachel: Myrt's in the bedroom. Take care of her, okay?

> Sandra: Of course. And the girls are really okay?

> Rachel: They are, but their phones are silenced while we finish up and I have to turn mine off too, for a little while. TTYS.

I silenced my phone, wincing when I did it. "She's gonna know I'm not telling the truth."

"What can she do?" Christy asked.

"Track my phone like we tracked Misty's."

Christy took my phone again, tapped, swiped, tapped, then handed it back. "Not anymore."

We got out of the car and cut through the woods alongside the field where the phone's location seemed to be. There was a culvert at the end where it went right under the road. We moved slowly, stepping soft in the underbrush. The sky was starting to turn from dark blue to light gray. It would be daylight soon.

Then we heard voices and came to a stop.

"Oh good, you're here," Jen Scott was saying, and I realized Jeremy had made it to her. "Now toss your gun down, and I'll take you to your girlfriend."

MISTY

Misty pressed up onto her hands and knees and crawled out of the culvert, into the tall grasses and wildflowers of the meadow. Her chest screamed. She was pretty sure she had a couple of broken ribs. When she inhaled, it felt like knives in her chest. But there was not a bullet in her heart. She wasn't dead. She was alive. And as long as she was alive, she wouldn't let that horrible Jen Scott hurt Jeremy. If she'd already done anything to Christy or to Rachel or Mason—the thought choked her and she had to pause, lower her head, and force herself to breathe again. If she'd hurt any of them, she was going to pay.

She couldn't stand up. If she did, she'd be seen. The sky was paling, so she crawled on hands and knees through the tall grasses, heading back toward where Jen had left her car, and praying it would still be there.

It was!

She slowed down, moving with more care, ignoring the pain. The chain was still around her neck, with her savior, the mermaid, hanging from it, her middle flattened by a bullet.

Every time Misty shifted her weight from arm to arm, the pain was a hot blade through her chest. Yet she moved steadily closer. Jen's car was there.

Her muscles gave out and she fell, and her chest hit the ground, the steel mermaid pressing again to the raw place in her chest, and it was beyond pain. She felt split in two.

She went rigid, trying to breathe, waiting for the pain to

ease. It took a long time. But then it ebbed and, as it did, their voices came to her.

"Oh Good, you're here. Now toss your gun down and I'll take you to your girlfriend."

Misty pushed herself up. Through the waving grasses, she could see them, Jen Scott, facing away from her, and Jeremy, facing toward her. She saw his beautiful face and her chest ached in a different way.

Jen Scott pointed her gun at Jeremy and said, "Your weapon?"

Misty crawled closer, her hands pressing to the soft grasses without a sound.

Jeremy raised his hands and said, "I'm not armed. I came out here to visit my girlfriend at college. I couldn't bring a gun."

She crept even closer. She was only feet away from them now.

"That should make this easier then," Jen Scott said, and she moved, and Misty knew she was going to shoot.

She closed her fist around the mermaid so it wouldn't slam into her chest as she lunged upright and forward. She shouted, not a word, but something more feral as she leapt, raising her arm over her head. The chain around her neck snapped. Misty brought the mermaid down on Jen Scott's neck, missed and hit her shoulder. The tail fins sank deep, though. Jen Scott screamed, yanked the mermaid from her neck and flung it to the ground. "What the—" and she looked from her shoulder, back at Misty. "I thought I killed you!"

Jeremy lunged, grabbed Jen from behind and took her

gun right out of her hand. She tried to wrestle free and fell down onto one knee.

"You stay down there," he said, holding the gun not quite on her, but close enough. He kept shifting his gaze to Misty, then back to Jen again. "I see you brought your handcuffs along," he said with a nod at the detective's hip. She was kneeling, holding her shoulder. It was gushing blood, and Misty wondered if she'd hit an artery.

"I can't cuff up," Jen said. "Not with this shoulder."

He moved to her, took the handcuffs out, put them on her good wrist, and pulled it around behind her back. Then he reached for her other arm.

It happened in an instant. Jen twisted, and suddenly there was a little gun in her other hand, and she shrieked, "Eva was mine. She belonged with me!"

Misty surged, slamming Jeremy with both hands. He hit the ground, and she landed on top of him as the gun went off. Even though she braced for the bullet, she never felt it. And then she realized as Jen dropped to the ground beside them, that she hadn't been aiming at Jeremy. She'd brought the little pistol's barrel up to her own chin.

"Oh, my God," she whispered.

"Holy fuck, Misty!" Christy came running across the field.

"Christy?" Then as her sister barreled into her, snapping her arms around her, "Oh, my God, you're alive! You're okay!"

They hugged so hard Misty winced in pain and pulled away, touching her chest softly. Mason and Rachel had appeared, as well. She didn't know where they'd come from, but she was glad to see them in one piece. The terror that had covered her heart in ice seemed to shatter and fall away.

"How the hell did you get out of the tank?" she asked her sister, stepping back just enough to look at her face.

"The Crisis Companion," Christy said, through her tears.

"You've gotta be kidding me." Misty looked at the ground where she'd seen Jen Scott throw her mermaid. She spotted it and went to pick it up. It still had blood on it, but she wasn't leaving it behind. She held it up in front of Christy.

The sun was rising, and it illuminated the mermaid with the round flat piece of lead in her belly. All her inner tools were mashed together. They'd flattened.

"Holy shit," Christy said, running her thumb over the metal. "Is that—?"

"A bullet, yeah." She pulled her blouse open, and everyone gathered around as the sunrise painted her flesh. On her sternum, between her breasts, was the perfect shape of a mermaid, stamped into her skin, cut into it in multiple places.

Christy laid her fingers on the mark.

"I think my ribs are broken," Misty said.

"That's okay," Christy replied, pointing to the stitches in her own head. "I know a few people at the hospital."

CHAPTER 15

RACHEL

My headpiece was a spray of fragrant apple blossoms, and my sister adjusted it seventeen times before she was satisfied. We were in the house, right at the front door, which was wide open. The kids were lined up outside. Jeremy was first, with Misty. Joshua, who was back from his cross-country adventure looking tanned and happy and older somehow, walked with Christy. As the music began, Jere and Misty started their slow walk down the front lawn, over the longest stretch of red carpet I'd ever seen. It unrolled between two sections of folding chairs, all the way to the shore, where there was a white garden arch decked in flowers, built by my perfect brother-in-law Jim. The officiant we'd hired, a round, happy woman with short white hair, awaited us there, her face alight.

I stood with Sandra, very close. As she fussed over my dress and hair, and the kids moved out from in front of us down the aisle, I could finally see Mason, waiting for me at the end. He looked so good in his black suit and black tie, with a single red rose bud on his lapel. He couldn't keep the smile from his face. I saw him trying. God, I loved that man. The dogs sat on either side of him. Myrtle had a little head piece that matched mine, and Hugo wore a top hat with a red rosebud. I looked at them and smiled, gave a tiny wave, and Myrtle barked.

We'd got her test results the very morning after returning from our wild weekend getaway-slash-murder-investigation. Dr. Hwang said that Myrtle's optic nerves were healing. She was getting her eyesight back. When I asked how that could be, his scientific reply was, "It just happens sometimes." Those fugue states when she would just go still and stare, were because she'd been gradually seeing more and more. Her independent streak increased the better her vision had become. And I was pretty sure she could see me right then, from the other end this happiest of walks. She was smiling almost as widely as Mason was.

Misty and Jeremy reached the front and took their places on either side of Mason and the dogs. Josh and Christy had made it halfway. Both girls were fully recovered and in possession of hefty cash settlements from the bad boy billionaires, who didn't want to be sued for unsafe work conditions. All the merfolk got checks, plus paid vacation while The Sapphire Club was undergoing repairs.

Josh and Christy reached the front and turned to face us.

Josh gave me a thumbs-up and a wink. He'd let his hair go shaggy. I liked it.

Sandra kissed my cheek. She'd pulled this wedding together in just two weeks' time, and everything seemed perfect so far. I thought she could do it for a living. I'd even suggest a name for her service: Short Notice Nuptials.

She was all teary-eyed, and that made me teary-eyed too.

"Don't cry. You'll smudge your makeup." She dabbed my cheek with one of the tissues she had handy.

"Do you forgive me?" I asked. "For not calling you sooner?"

"I forgive you," she said. "But that doesn't mean it's okay. It's not okay. You should've called."

I nodded. "It was bizarre, how you bought them mermaids, not knowing—"

"Moms and daughters are connected more than just physically," she said, then shrugged one shoulder. "Besides, you dreamed about mermaids not knowing."

"I do that, though. And those ugly-ass mermaids you bought saved their lives."

She smiled the way a fox smiled when it discovered an unprotected flock of chickens. I mean, probably. I'd never seen a fox discover an unprotected flock of chickens, but one assumes. "They can't give me any of their bullshit for at least, what? A year, you think?"

"At least," I agreed. "No backtalk, no guilt trips."

"No ignoring texts or not visiting." She took a big, satisfied breath. "You look beautiful."

I felt like a Greek goddess in my dress.

Sandra gave me a final hug, then walked out ahead of me. I stood back from the open door a little bit, in the shadows, as she had instructed. When she made it to the front, the music changed to "The Bridal March." I met Mason's eyes as I walked toward him. I tried to go slow, but honestly, I couldn't wait to be his wife.

I reached the front, and he took my hands and gazed into my eyes while our officiant said the words. The reservoir was behind us, and our beautiful family before us, looking on as we repeated the simple, traditional vows.

Everyone we loved was there, and half the Binghamton PD with their spouses and partners. Misty's mermaid friends were there. They were going to pose for photos with the guests at the reception— the best party favor ever, according to Sandra.

When finally asked the key question, I looked into my gorgeous man's eyes and said "I do. I really, fuckin' do."

He squeezed my hands and laughed softly. I saw a tear shimmering in the corner of his eye and my heart turned to mush.

"I fuckin' do, too," he said, when it was his turn.

Then we wrapped ourselves around each other and kissed, and I knew that everything had changed. I hadn't expected it to. I'd thought this was just a ceremony to formalize what we already had. But it was more. It was magical. It took everything to a whole new level.

I clung a little tighter to his neck as his lips moved over mine, and then he pulled me close, and whispered, "You good?"

"So good."

We turned to face the family as the officiant pronounced us husband and wife, and everyone cheered. I smiled so hard I thought my face might break.

Taking my hand, Mason led me back up the aisle as flower petals were tossed at our heads. But instead of heading to the big, white tent on the side lawn, where the reception was about to get underway, he led me away from the crowd and down to the water's edge.

We stood there together. I was gorgeous in my stunning dress, and he was fire in his dark suit.

"I didn't think I could love you more," he said. "But today..."

"Yeah, yeah. Get all sappy on me." I clasped his hands, and he pulled them to his lips. "Same, though," I said. "I feel just the same."

Something caught my eye past him, out in the water. The mermaid! Eva! She waved, and I felt a rush of joy wash over me. It wasn't organic, though I had plenty of that. It felt like Eva's joy, as if she'd beamed it out. Then she arched like a dolphin and vanished with a splash of her blue and silver tail.

"Seeing mermaids again?" Mason asked softly. He turned, sliding an arm around my shoulders and looking right where I was looking.

"Just the one," I said.

"Eva's funeral was today," Mason reminded me. "They put her next to Paul."

I nodded. "She's okay. At peace. She might even get to be a mermaid in the afterlife."

"Yeah?" Mason asked, eyebrows up.

I loved that he never acted like the crazy shit I said was crazy at all. "Yeah," I said. "She's happy. And so am I."

"Me too, babe." He swept me into his arms for a romantic kiss. The sun sank over the reservoir, and life was good.

BROWN AND DE LUCA

Vist: MaggieShayne.com for more information.

ABOUT THE AUTHOR

New York Times and *USA Today* bestselling novelist Maggie Shayne has published 112 novels and novellas for numerous major publishers. She also spent a year writing for American daytime TV dramas *The Guiding Light* and *As the World Turns*. But her heart was in her books, and she'd found it impossible to do both.

Now, she is excited to be publishing with dream-publisher, Oliver Heber Books and she's having more fun than ever.

Maggie lives in a century-and-a-half old farmhouse with two waterfalls outside, in the rural hills of Cortland County NY with her husband Lance, who builds waterfalls for a living, and their dogs. There are always, always dogs.

facebook.com/MaggieShayneAuthor

instagram.com/MaggieShayne

threads.net/@maggieshayne

bookbub.com/authors/maggie-shayne

amazon.com/author/maggieshayne

Printed in the USA
CPSIA information can be obtained
at www.ICGtesting.com
CBHW021050140724
11573CB00004B/96

9 781648 395581